GHOST

Run: Book 1

JASON REYNOLDS

Published by the Knights Of
Knights Of Ltd, Registered Offices:
119 Marylebone Road, London, NW1 5PU

www.knightsof.media
First published 2018
001

Written by Jason Reynolds
Text and cover copyright © Jason Reynolds, 2018
Cover art by © Selom Sunu, 2018
First published in the USA by Atheneum,
an imprint of Simon and Schuster, Inc, 2016
All rights reserved
The moral right of the author and illustrator has been asserted

Set in ITC Stone Serif / 12 pt
Design and Typeset by Marssaié Jordan
Printed and bound in the UK

A CIP catalogue record for this book
will be available from the British Library

ISBN: 978-1-9996425-2-5

2 4 6 8 10 9 7 5 3 1

to the runners

GHOST

"Let me guess, sunflower seeds," Mr Charles practically shouts from behind the counter of what he calls his "country store," even though we live in a city. Mr Charles, who, by the way, looks just like James Brown if James Brown were white, has been ringing me up for sunflower seeds five days a week for about, let me think . . . since fourth grade, which is when Ma took the hospital job. So for about three years now. He's also hard of hearing, which when my mum used to say this, I always thought she was saying "harder hearing," which made no sense at all to me. I don't know why she just didn't say "almost deaf." Maybe because "hard of hearing" is more like hospital talk, which was probably rubbing off on her. But, yeah, Mr Charles can barely hear a thing, which is why he's always yelling at everybody and everybody's always yelling at him. His store is a straight-up scream fest, not to mention the extra sound effects from the loud TV he keeps behind the counter – cowboy movies on repeat. Mr Charles is also the guy who gave me this book, *Guinness World Records*, which is where I found out about Andrew Dahl and Charlotte Lee. He tells me I can set a record one day. A real record. Be one of the world's greatest somethings. Maybe. But I know one thing, Mr Charles has to hold the record for saying, *Let me guess, sunflower seeds*, because he says that every single time I come in, which means I probably also already hold the record for responding, loudly, the exact same way.

"Let me guess, one dollar." That's my comeback. Said it a gazillion times. Then I slap a coin in the palm of his wrinkly hand, and he puts the bag of seeds in mine.

After that, I continue on my slow-motion journey, pausing again only when I get to the bus stop. But this bus stop isn't just any bus stop. It's the one that's directly across the street from the gym. I just sit there with the other people waiting for the bus, except I'm never actually waiting for it. The bus gets you home fast, and I don't want that. I just go there to look at the people working out. See, the gym across the street has this big window – like the whole wall is a window – and they have those machines that make you feel like you walking up steps and so everybody just be facing the bus stop, looking all crazy like they're about to pass out.

3

And trust me, there isn't anything funnier than that. So I check that out for a little while like it's some kind of movie: *The About to Pass Out Show*, starring stair-stepper person one through ten. I know this all probably sounds kind of weird, maybe even creepy, but it's something to do when you're bored. Best part about sitting there is tearing into my sunflower seeds like they're theatre popcorn.

About the sunflower seeds. I used to just put a whole bunch of them in my mouth at the same time, suck all the salt off, then spit them all out machine-gun-style. I could've probably set a world record in that, too. But now, I've matured. Now I take my time, moving them around, positioning them for the perfect bite to pop open the shell, then carefully separating the seed from it with my tongue, then – and this is the hard part – keeping the little seed safe in the space between my teeth and tongue, I spit the shells out. And finally, after all that, I chew the seed up. I'm like a master at it, even though, honestly, sunflower seeds don't taste like nothing. I'm not even sure they're really worth all the hassle. But I like the process anyway.

My dad used to eat sunflower seeds too.

That's where I get it from. But he used to chew the whole thing up. The shells, the seeds, everything. Just devour them like some kind of beast. When I was really young, I used to ask him if a sunflower was going to grow inside of him since he ate the seeds so much. He was always watching some kind of game, like football or basketball, and he'd turn to me just for a second, just long enough to not miss a play, and say, "Sunflowers are all up in me, kid." Then he'd shake up the seeds in his palm like dice, before throwing another bunch in his mouth to chomp down on.

But let me tell you, my dad was lying. Wasn't no sunflowers growing in him. Couldn't have been. I don't know a whole lot about sunflowers, but I know they're pretty and girls like them, and I know the word sunflower is made up of two good words, and that man hasn't got two good words in him, or anything that any girl would like, because girls don't like men who try to shoot them and their son. And that's the kind of man he was.

It was three years ago when my dad lost it. When the alcohol made him meaner than he'd ever been. Every other night he would become a different person, like he'd morph into someone crazy, but this one night my mother decided to finally fight back. This one night everything went worse. I had my head sandwiched between the mattress and my pillow, something I got used to doing whenever they were going at it, when my mum crashed into my bedroom.

"We gotta go," she said, pulling the covers off the bed. And when I didn't move fast enough, she yelled, "Come on!"

Next thing I knew, she was dragging me down the hallway, my feet tripping over themselves. And that's when I looked back and saw him, my dad, staggering from the bedroom, his lips bloody, a pistol in his hand.

"Don't make me do this, Terri!" he angry-begged, but me and my mum kept rolling. The sound of the gun cocking. The sound of the door unlocking. As soon as she swung the door open, my dad fired a shot. He was shooting at us! My dad! My dad was actually shooting . . . at . . . US! His wife and his boy! I didn't look to see what he hit, mainly because I was scared it was gonna be me. Or Ma. The sound was big, and sharp enough to make me feel like my brain was gonna pop in my head, enough to make my heart hiccup.

But the craziest thing was, I felt like the shot – loudest sound I ever heard – made my legs move even faster. I don't know if that's possible, but that's definitely what it seemed like.

My mum and I kept running, down the staircase into the street, breaking into the darkness with death chasing behind us. We ran and ran and ran, until finally we came up on Mr Charles's store, which, luckily for us, stays open 24/7. Mr Charles took one look at me and my mum, out of breath, crying, barefoot in our pyjamas, and hid us in his storage room while he called the cops. We stayed there all night.

I haven't seen my dad since. Ma said the police said that when they got to the house, he was sitting outside on the steps, shirtless, with the pistol beside him, guzzling beer, eating sunflower seeds, waiting. Like he wanted to get caught. Like it was no big deal. They gave him ten years in prison, and to be honest, I don't know if I'm happy about that or not. Sometimes, I wish he'd got forever in jail. Other times, I wish he was home on the couch, watching the game, shaking seeds in his hand. Either way, one thing is for sure: that was the night I learned how to run. So when I was done sitting at the bus stop in front of the gym, and came across all those kids on the track at the park, practising, I had to go see what was going on, because running isn't anything I ever had to practise. It's just something I knew how to do.

2

WORLD RECORD FOR THE FASTEST TRY-OUT EVER

AT FIRST I watched through the gate. I was gonna keep moving, but then I saw that there were other people down closer to the track, hanging out, watching the practise. Like mums and stuff. So I joined them. Well, I didn't sit *with them,* because that would've been weird, but I grabbed a seat on one of the other benches. My school didn't have a track team, not that I would've tried out for it if it did. I was more into basketball. That was my sport, even though I had never really played. Sometimes on my walk home I would stop at the court and see if I could get a pickup game, but no one ever picked me, mainly because the old heads didn't like running with kids my age. But I always had this feeling that if I could just get on, I'd be the next LeBron. But I never wanted to be the next . . . whoever the most famous runner is. I never even thought about it. I looked in the world records book and it says some guy named Usain Bolt is the fastest, but I had never heard of him. My dad never watched *running* on TV. Are there even any famous runners? Like, seriously? I never heard of none, but judging from the way these kids were stretching and jumping around on the track, some of them probably had.

"Okay, let's get some high knees!" the coach was commanding. He was short, and bald, but I could tell that his baldy didn't come from all his hair falling out. He was one of those guys who shaved it. Actually, he was one of those guys who shaved all the hair on his face except his eyebrows, which wasn't a good look. He looked like a turtle. A turtle with a chipped tooth, wearing a hoop earring and a black whistle around his neck. "Up! Up! Up!"

There were boys and girls – around my age – everybody dressed in shorts and T-shirts, holding their arms out in front of them, doing a jump-march kind of thing, slapping their knees to their hands.

"Come on, Sunny! It's only the second

day of practise and you're already slackin'!" the coach barked at the tallest boy out there. He was holding a clipboard and smacked it against his leg. "Get 'em up!"

I sat with my feet spread apart so I could spit the sunflower-seed shells on the ground between them. The salt was making me so thirsty, but I just couldn't stop eating them. On the track, the high-knee things were followed by jumping jacks, and some warm-up laps around the track, which seemed like a really bad idea to me. I mean, why would you run to warm up? You'd be tired before it's even time to race. *Duh.* Then all the runners gathered around the turtle-faced coach.

"Listen up," he said. "If you are on this track, you have either already been part of the Defenders, or you have been recruited to be part of the Defenders." He was talking to them like they had just joined the army or something. "I'm sure you all know what that means, but in case you don't, it means that you are part of one of the best youth teams in the city. We are the people the top high schools come to for talent.

And if you go to a good high school and do well on a good team, guess what? You might even get to go to college for free."

Don't nobody go to college for free to run no races, I thought to myself, spitting a shell out. I hate when they get stuck to your tongue and you gotta do that spit-flick thing. So annoying.

A weird-looking kid, I can't really explain what he looked like, well . . . let me try. You know how I said Mr Charles looked like James Brown if James Brown was white? Well, this kid looked like a white boy, if a white boy was black. Wait. That doesn't make sense. Let me start over. His skin was white. Like, the colour white. And his hair was light brown. But his face looked like a black person's. Like God forgot to put the brown in him. Wait, is that like Mr Charles or not? Forget it. Anyway, the boy raised his hand.

"Yes, Lu?" the coach said.

"Is it true you ran in the Olympics?" the kid asked.

"Is it true that you didn't?" the coach shot back, playing him out.

The boy called Lu stood there like he just got slapped in the face by one of Charlotte Lee's rubber ducks. Like he didn't know what to do. "U-uh . . . ," he stammered, not sure of what to say.

"Don't worry about what *I've* done. Worry about what *you* want to do. If you stick with me, I can get you there." The coach wiped spit from the corners of his mouth. "Now," he said, looking at his register, "let's see what we can do with you newbies. Lu, Patina, Sunny, on the line!"

The three "newbies" hustled down to the other end of the track.

"Lu, you're up first. Hundred metre on the whistle," the coach directed. The weird-looking guy, Lu, was decked out in the flyest gear. Fresh Nike running shoes, and a full-body skintight suit. Like a superhero. He wore a headband and a gold chain around his neck, and a diamond glinted in each ear. All the other runners stood off to the side as the coach put the whistle in his mouth. He held a stopwatch in his other hand. "Ready," he said through his teeth. Then came the short squeak, *badeep!* and Lu took off.

It was quick. I mean, this kid was really fast, and when he got to the end of the straightaway, a woman who was sitting on a bench on the other side of the track jumped up and squealed and clapped like this guy was some kind of celebrity or something. I was impressed, not enough to clap – really, I was just happy something unboring was *finally* happening – but definitely impressed enough to stop sorting seeds in my mouth until he was done.

"Nice job," the coach said as Lu trotted back over to the side like a pro. Like this was no big deal, and he knew it. He glanced over at me. I spit shells on the ground. The coach also called out a time and scribbled it down, but I didn't catch it.

Next up was the big goofy-looking kid the coach called Sunny. He was the one getting yelled at when I first got there about not kicking his legs up high enough in the warm-up. To be honest, he didn't look like he could even walk in a straight line, so I figured this was going to be pretty funny. Sunny got in position, closed his eyes, and took slow, deep breaths. Then the coach blew the whistle, and off he went. I could tell he was pushing as hard as he could, but he just wasn't going nowhere. It was like he was running into the wind, even though it wasn't a windy day. Like his shoes weighed a ton or his bones were heavy or something. Nobody cheered for him, and a few of the other kids even laughed.

"We'll see who's laughing when we get to the mile," the coach barked at the sniggering runners. They all cut it out quick. Sunny loped back over and joined the group, unfazed. He didn't even mind that he had run the slowest I had ever seen anyone run. His sprint was like a jog. My mother could've probably smoked him. Mr Charles might've even burned him up, and he's like a thousand years old! The coach gave Sunny a nod, then turned to the next person. A girl. "Next up, Patina."

The Patina girl was tall, and sprang up and down on her toes, rolling her neck and shoulders, I guessed to loosen up. Her hair was yanked back in a stubby ponytail, with lots of frizz around the edges. When the coach blew the whistle, Patina broke out in a flash, zooming down the track definitely faster than Sunny, but not quite as fast as Lu. Still, I was impressed. I mean, I don't know a whole bunch of girls who can run that fast. Actually, I don't really know a whole bunch of girls who run at all. They always be trying to be cute in school, but I'm not mad about that.

"Y'all vets better look out for this girl. She runs the eight hundred like it's a skip down the road," the coach said, giving Patina a high five. If anybody complimented me like that, I'd be trying hard not to smile, but would probably slip a little one in. But she, Patina, she just kept it cool and got back in line like it was nothing. I could tell she was no joke.

After Lu, Sunny, and Patina ran, the coach told all the other runners, "the vets," to line up and show "the newbies" how it was done. So on and on it went, the whistle blowing, one by one, boys and girls on the line, sprinting down the straightaway. Each of their times being recorded. Some were faster than others. Actually, most of the vets were pretty fast, but nobody was faster than the pretty boy, Lu. Nobody. And the coach kept saying stuff like, "Lu's still the one to beat," which was kind of pissing me off because . . .
I don't know. It just made me think about this kid Brandon at school, who always . . . ALWAYS

picked on me. Not even just me, though. He picked on a lot of people, and didn't nobody ever do nothing about it. They just said stupid stuff like, *Can't nobody beat him.* Same kind of rah-rah this bowling-ball-head coach was kicking about this kid, Lu. It's just . . . ugh. I mean, he was fast, but honestly, he wasn't *that* fast.

When everyone had taken a turn, the coach started over and gave everybody a chance to give it another go to see if they could beat their first time. So Lu was up for another go. He did that same cocky swagger over to the starting line. Did a few stretches, some jumps. And the lady on the other side of the track screamed again. The boy was just getting loose and she was going off like he was doing something. The people around her looked at her like she was crazy, obviously annoyed. All of his teammates looked on. Some of them seemed to be bubbling with anticipation to see the mighty Lu run again. Others looked . . . over it. That's probably how I looked. That's definitely how I felt. Over Lu, over Brandon, and over anybody else who thought they were unbeatable. Not to mention I was all out of sunflower seeds, so I had nothing to hold me back from getting up and showing him that he really wasn't all that, and that I ain't never had a running lesson in my whole life and I could keep up with him, if not beat him. So I stepped over all the sunflower seed shells that had piled up between my feet like a mountain of dead flies, and walked, not on the track, but just beside it, on the grass. I lined up with Lu, who had now dropped into his "on your mark" stance. I didn't need to do all that. I just needed to roll my jeans up and tuck my laces in my high-tops and I was good to go.

Coach Turtle Face noticed me and called out, "Kid, what are you doing? Tryouts were last week."

I didn't say nothing, and the coach followed up with, "This is a private practise."

I still didn't respond, and just started scrunching the sleeves of my T-shirt up to my shoulders.

"Did you hear me?" the coach now asked, a little louder this time. He started walking toward me. The other kids were looking at me like most kids did. Like I was something else.

Like I wasn't one of them. But whatever. "Do you not understand what *private* means?" the coach jeered. I thought of a funny comeback but kept it to myself.

"Yeah, man, the track is for runners, not people who want to *pretend* like they runners," Lu jabbed, now standing straight. He looked me up and down, then flashed an arrogant grin.

"Just blow the whistle!" I finally called back to the coach. He stopped in his tracks and glared. Then he looked at Lu before continuing in my direction. He pointed his clipboard at me.

"Listen, you get one run, hear me? After this, I don't want to see you around here no more," he threatened. "This is serious business, you understand?"

I gave him the *whatever* face and nodded. He pointed his stupid clipboard at me again, like I was scared of that. Please. Then, as the coach headed back to the finish line, Lu shook his head at me and growled, "Hope you ready to get smoked."

This time I said it. "Whatever," and gave him my best ice smile to make sure he knew he didn't scare me. And he didn't. We were just running, not fighting, so why should I be frightened by some milk-face running boy?

Now back at the other end of the track, the coach yelled out, "On your mark . . ." Lu dropped down on all fours again. I just put my right foot forward. "Get set . . ." Lu put his butt in the air. I leaned in. Then . . . *badeep!* I wish I could tell you what I was thinking. But I can't. I probably wasn't thinking nothing. Just moving. Man, were my legs going! I pumped and pushed, my ankles loose and wobbly in my trainers, my jeans stiff and hot, the whole time seeing Lu out the corner of my eye like a white blur. And then it was over. And everybody watching, all the other runners, clapped and hooted, pointing at us both. Some had their mouths open. Others just looked confused. The lady on the other side of the track – not a peep. But all the people around her were standing and cheering.

Lu walked in circles with his hands on his head, trying to catch his breath, panting, wheezing out, "Who won? Who won, Coach?"

"I don't know, son. It was pretty close." The coach said it like the words were sour in his mouth. I walked back over to my bench, grabbed my backpack, and to keep my part of the deal, headed out. I'd made my point, and it wasn't like I wanted to be part of their little club. I just needed everybody to know that the fancy, white-black boy wasn't all that.

"Kid." I could hear the coach's footsteps coming behind me. I was still trying to get my heart to stop trippin' and my lungs to start working again. "Kid, wait. Wait," he said, running up beside me. He was wearing those trousers, the swishy-swishy kind that make every step sound like paper crumpling. "Who you run for?" he asked. What? Who did I run for? What kind of question was that?

"I run for me. Who else?" I replied. I stopped walking.

"No, I mean, what team?"

"No team."

"I see." He glanced over at the track. "So then, who trained you? Somebody had to train you to be so fast."

"Nobody. I just know how to run."

"You just know how to run," he repeated under his breath, followed up by, "Yes. Yes, you do," also under his breath.

"Look, I don't know you—what's your name?"

"Castle Cranshaw," I said, then quickly clarified, "But everybody calls me Ghost." By everybody, I meant nobody except me. That was my self-given nickname. Well, halfway self-given. The night me and Ma busted into Mr Charles's store, Mr Charles looked at us like he was looking at two ghosts. Like he didn't recognise us, probably because of how scared we both must've looked. So I just started calling myself that. Plus it wasn't the only time someone had looked at me that way. As a matter of fact, this man, the coach, was looking at me the exact same way as Mr Charles did that night, stunned, and I couldn't tell if it was because my real name was Castle or because of my nickname.

"Okay . . . uh . . . Ghost. I'm Coach Brody." We did a proper handshake. "Listen, like I said, I don't know you, obviously, but I know you got something special. At least

I think you do. So, you want to join the Defenders and run with us?"

I didn't even think about it.

"Nope." Just like that.

"Nope?" Judging by the look on Coach's face, I could tell nobody said no to running on his team, ever. "What you mean, nope? Why not?"

All the other runners on the track were cracking jokes and playing around. Everybody but Lu. He was back on the line down on his knees, like he was getting ready to take off again.

"Because my sport is basketball."

"You play ball?" he asked, like he didn't believe it. Like I didn't look like I could hoop.

"Yep."

"For who?"

"Why you keep asking me who I do things for?" I snapped, mainly because I didn't play ball for nobody. Not yet, at least. But it was still in my plans. Plus, who was he to be all in my business anyway? I didn't even know him. And he didn't know me. "Look, even if I wanted to join your team," I continued, "I would have to ask my mother first, and she's probably gonna say no, so – "

"So let me ask her," he cut in.

"Why you care? It's just running," I said.

"Is that what you think?" Coach narrowed his eyes. "That this is just running?"

"Uh . . . yeah. I mean, what else is there? Ready, set, go. Run. The end," I said like a robot.

Coach let out a hearty laugh, the kind that sounds fake. Nobody really laughs that hard and that loud without bending over like it hurts. "We'll get to that," Coach said, cutting his laugh off instantly. Like I said, fake. "For now, let's focus on the task at hand. If your mum says it's cool, will you join?"

"Man, I told you, I play ball."

Coach sized me up, biting down on his bottom lip. "Okay, I'll tell you what. Basketball's your sport? Cool. But if you wanna be a better ball player, join this team and you'll be faster and stronger than anyone on any court. Matter fact, your legs will be so strong you'll be dunking on people by next year."

"You think I'm stupid?" I looked at him sideways. No way I could be dunking in a year. I never heard of no eighth graders that can dunk.

"Depends on what you say next. You are if you don't let me ask your mum about joining." Coach was looking at me like he was dead serious. Like he really thought running could help my hops and get me dunking by next year, which if that *did* happen, I would go right down to the court with Sicko and them and demand to play. I kept checking his face for a sign he was lying, a sign that would've been easy to see because he didn't have any hair to disguise it. But there was no sign. No lie.

"Man, I'm telling you, she isn't gonna say yes." "Good enough." Coach nodded, a sure smirk on his face. "Practise is almost over. Might as well stay, and then I'll drop you off at home. I'll talk to her then. Cool?"

Not cool. Not really. I mean, track? And who was this man? I've seen those weird shows where psychos pose like coaches and stuff and get you caught up and the next thing you know my mother's in jail too for handling this guy. I didn't trust him. But on the other hand, I didn't really have anything else to do, or nowhere else to be, so I figured it was worth scoping him out and seeing how he acted around all the other kids and their parents. I mean, I could always use the ride home, but I'm no fool.

After practise was done, everybody met up with the people waiting for them, family and friends or whatever. Coach spent a lot of time talking to all the mums and dads – mostly mums – especially of the vets. They all acted like they really, really knew each other. Like family. Hugs and all that. And that made me feel a little better about him, because mums don't trust nobody around their kids. So I agreed on the ride.

Coach and I walked to his car, which I was surprised to see was a cab.

"You stole a cab?" I asked, while he cleaned a bunch of stuff off the seat. Food bags, shoes, water bottles, sports drinks. The front of his car was a mess. He threw everything in the back.

"No," Coach said, brushing crumbs on the floor so I could finally get in. "What makes you think that?"

"Because you a coach," I said, holding my backpack in my lap. "So how you get one?"

"I coach because I love it. But it don't pay the rent. Being a cab driver does." He started the car.

"Then why would you love coaching? Seems like if being a cabbie gets you paid, that should be what you love," I explained what seemed obvious, looking out the window. Coach backed out of the parking space.

"Wait," I said. "You not gonna make me pay for this ride home, are you? Because if you are, you can just let me out and I can walk."

"Why would I make – " Coach started, then stopped. Then he sighed. "Just tell me where you live."

Where I live. Where I live. When anyone ever asks about where I live, I get weird because people always treat you funny when they find out you stay in a certain kind of neighbourhood. But I was used to people treating me funny. When your clothes are two sizes too big, and you got on no-name trainers, and your mother cuts your hair and it looks like your mother cuts your hair, you get used to people treating you funny. So what's one more person?

"Glass Manor," I said. "You know where that's at?"

Coach didn't blink. "Yeah, I know where that is."

We didn't really say too much in the car. Just zipped from one side of the neighbourhood to the other – from the good side to the "other" side. It was my first time ever in a cab. I was used to walking everywhere, unless I was going somewhere with my mum. Then it was on the bus. Coach talked on the phone most of the trip. Judging by what he was saying, what time he'd be home, checking to see if somebody named Tyrone had eaten yet, asking what was for dinner, made me think he was talking to his wife. I wonder what she looked like. Probably not too hot, since she married a man who looked like a chipped-tooth turtle. Coach was saying something about gym shoes to the maybe-wife on the phone when I noticed a woman walking in white scrubs, white trainers, carrying a black leather purse big enough to fit the whole world in it, and her hair was cut like a boy's. I tapped Coach on the arm and told him to pull the cab over.

"Hold on," he said to the person on the phone. Then to me, "What?"

"Pull over," I repeated. "That's my mother."

Coach pulled to the side of the street, and I rolled down the window. "Ma!" I called out, waving to her.

She looked, then looked again, trying to make sure I was who she thought I was.

"Cas?" she said, approaching the cab. "What are you doing in a cab? Matter fact, what are you doing in the front seat of a cab? No, answer the first question. What are you doing in a cab?"

"Hop in," I said.

"No, you hop out," she replied.

"Ma."

"Ma'am." Coach leaned over so she could see him. "It's fine. Hop in. I'm just giving him a ride home." Then he added, "On the house."

Coach swiped everything on the backseat to one side as I reached back and opened the door. My mother stood outside the car for what seemed like minutes before deciding to climb in. And even after she did, she kept the door open, one foot still on the pavement, so she could jump back out if she needed to. Her bag, which

I knew was full of plastic containers of chicken and gravy, or whatever gross but free meal we were going to be having for dinner, crunched on the seat beside her as she finally pulled her leg in and closed the door.

"How was work?" I asked as Coach pulled back into the street.

"Cas, don't 'how was work' me. Why are you in a cab? And excuse me, sir, no offence, but who are you?" she asked. Told you. Mums don't trust nobody around their kids.

Coach adjusted the rearview mirror so he could see my mother in the back.

"I'm Coach Brody, but everybody calls me Coach. I run the Defenders city track team."

"Uh-huh. And?"

"And your son came and, uh, sat in on my practise today." Coach threw a quick glance at me. "Did you know he could run?"

"Did I know he could run?" She was sitting directly behind me, but I could still feel the heat of her eyes burning through the headrest, scorching the back of my neck.

"Yeah, he can run. Like, *really* run."

My mother just sort of grunted. I knew

better than to say anything, or to even turn around and look back at her. I just said to Coach, "Make this left," when we got close to my street.

Coach made the left and continued, "And I think he's got potential. With the proper coaching, he could be a serious problem." I felt like I had seen this in every single sports movie I had ever watched. All of them. *Ma'am, your son has potential.* If this went like the movies, I was either going to score the game-winning touchdown (which is impossible) or . . . die.

"Sir, I appreciate that, but let me tell you something. Cas already is a serious problem," my mum explained. "And right now, he needs to focus on school, not sports."

"Right here," I murmured to let Coach know where to stop and let us out. I figured there was no reason to drag the conversation out. It went exactly like I thought it would. So I wasn't really even mad about it. He cut his blinker on, pulled over, and put the car in park.

"Listen" – Coach turned around to look my mother in the face – "I totally get that. But what if I made you a deal," he went on. "If he messes up in school, one time, he's off the team."

"One time?!" I squawked.

"One time." Coach held his hand out to my mother. I kept my eyes forward until I heard her exhale the breath of a long day.

"You're gonna get him home every day?" she asked.

"Yes."

"What about his homework?"

"It'll be done." He sounded pretty confident for not even knowing me like that.

Coach gave us both one of his cards. I put mine in my bag while Ma gazed at hers, making sure everything was legit. Then she let out another big sigh, this time probably the breath of a worried mum.

"Well, at least I'll know where he'll be after school," she gave in.

And that was it. Just like that. For the first time in my whole life, I was on a team.

3

WORLD RECORD FOR THE MOST ALTERCATIONS

WHAT DO THEY call criminal records? Not criminal records. They call them something else. Rap sheets? Yeah, that's it, rap sheets, which is such a dumb name because it makes me think of rap music, like maybe a rap sheet is what rappers write their rhymes down on. But yeah, rap sheets. I got one of those. Not a real one, though, one that real criminals have, nah. I got a school rap sheet, but in school they call it a "file." I got a file. And even though I've never actually seen it, it has to be pretty big, because I'm always being sent down to the principal's office, or put in detention, or suspended for shutting people down for talking smack. *Oh, Castle, why your clothes so big? Why your pants so small? Why your name Castle? Why you always smell like you walked a thousand miles to get here? Why it look like somebody tried to cut your hair with a butter knife?* And my response would be . . . well, let's just use the school-y terms – "not exemplary behaviour." But I'd made a decision that there would be no more entries added to the file. The file would be closed forever, because now my new career in track, which was really my soon-to-be career in basketball, was at stake. All of a sudden I had too much on the line. There would be no more "altercations." That's the word Principal Marshall always used on the phone with my mother. *Altercations.*

And I was altercation free . . . for seventeen hours and two minutes. Two of those hours were spent watching one of those corny, romantic, mushy-mushy movies with my mum. She loves those things, and every night when we're eating dinner, she sits on our couch in the living room and watches one while opening mail and cutting out vouchers. I always spread all my blankets out on the floor – three or four to make what Ma calls a pallet – which is where I eventually doze off. She takes the couch. We haven't slept in our rooms since . . . Dad. It's too weird for her

(8:47 a.m.) Forty-five minutes in English class, where we were reading *Lord of the Flies*, which, by the way, is a crazy book (10:00 a.m.) Then forty-five minutes in math class, which was basically forty-five minutes of Maureen Thorne raising her hand every single time Mr Granger asked a question so that she could go up to the board and write the answer. Such a show-off. She's like the geeky girl version of Lu. So yeah, that happened (10:50 a.m.) And then there was social studies class, which I usually call nap time because we never study nothing social. Like . . . I don't know, social media. Or social events, like parties. All social studies is, is a stupid way to say "history." It's like the "rap sheet" of history. Or something like that. Anyway, I would usually snooze through it, but it was a new day and I was turning over a new leaf, so I stayed awake. Didn't really focus too much on nothing being said, but my eyes were wide open (11:40 a.m.)

And then lunch. You know who ate lunch the same time I did? Brandon Simmons. Jack from *Lord of the Flies*. A power-hungry dummy and the single most annoying guy in the seventh grade. He owned that record, a record that's really hard to own because there are a lot of annoying dummies in the seventh grade. Trust me, I know. But none like him. Brandon was a year older than everybody, because he stayed back a year. Guy was as dumb as dirt, and that wouldn't have been so bad if he was at least cool, but he wasn't. Plus he was taller than most of us, so he treated everybody like chumps. Especially me.

Just made it to the cafeteria (11:44 a.m.) Got in line. Brandon came in after me, bumped me, and then, seeing that I ignored him, decided to step in front of me.

"Shack," he said. Shack was what he called me as his lame way of making fun of the fact that my name is Castle. "You don't mind me butting in front of you, right? I mean, it's not like you haven't had cafeteria food before. You probably had some last night, right?" He shrugged and hit me with another one. "Right?" The only reason Brandon even knew about my mother is back when we were in the fourth grade – yes, I've known him that long – my mother thought it would be a good idea to come speak at Career Day. And Brandon has used it as fuel ever since.

He grinned, then looked around to make sure other people had heard him, which was always the most important part of his jerkness. Then a few more. "Right? Right?"

I sat at the table (11:50 a.m.) The same table I sat at every day with my two friends Dre Anderson and Red Griffin. I met Dre this year, and we hit it off because he's a ballplayer too. Plays for the Boys and Girls Club, and he told me I should've played, but I missed the tryouts. On purpose. Thing is, Boys and Girls Clubs don't ever really cut nobody. Everybody can just sign up and play, but who wants to be on a team with a bunch of pityplayers? I didn't wanna bust Dre's bubble because that isn't cool. But for me, I'm too good to play on a team like that. I mean, I didn't really know that, but . . . I knew that, y'know?

And Red, well, I've known him for a long time. We've been cool since fifth grade, mainly because even though we've never really talked about nothing bad, we both kind of knew something bad had happened to us. Like, for me, the best way to describe it is, I got a lot of scream inside. And I could tell Red did too. He was a white boy with red hair who everybody was friends with mainly because people were scared that he was crazy and it's better to be on crazy's good side. Jessica Grant said her mother said the only reason people have red hair is because they're red on the inside. Red like violent. But I got black hair, so does that mean I'm black on the inside? Anyway, Brandon came and sat next to Red at the table. He usually sat further down by the other gas-mouths, but not today. Today he sat right next to Red, and right across from me and Dre.

"Yo, Red, you ever been to Glass Manor?" Brandon asked while chomping on a chicken drummy.

"Nope," Red said, dry, just before taking a sip of his juice. He wasn't paying Brandon no mind.

"Oh man, you should go. It's something to see," Brandon said, now looking right at me. We caught eyes for a second, but then I darted mine to my fries and ketchup. Dip, then bite. Dip, then bite. Don't look up. *Don't pay him no attention.* Dip. Then. Bite. Brandon continued, "You really get to see where they got the name

Glass Manor from, because dude, everybody who lives around there is freakin' shattered."

Dre let out a big sigh, like a *here we go again* sigh, and Red glanced at me because he knew I lived there. Everybody knew I lived there, and even though I wasn't the only kid at school from that neighbourhood, it seemed like I caught the most mess about it. At least from Brandon. Red looked back at Brandon, disgusted, then went on eating. What a dumb joke.

Brandon was talking to Monique, who sat next to him (12:02 p.m.) Really he was snatching food off her plate and teasing her about her acne. But the thing was, everybody knew he had a crush on Monique, no matter how many moon-face jokes he cracked. Everybody also knew that he tried to get her, but she kept rejecting him, which was the real reason he snapped on her. Her acne wasn't even all that bad.

"Hey, Shack," he called out. "All you gonna have is fries?" Again, I didn't say nothing. I didn't have to explain that I always got just fries so I could save a dollar to get sunflower seeds later. So I just ignored him. Just sat there with my empty tray and shook up my chocolate milk. Lunch would be over in a few minutes. A few minutes. I was so close. So close. Then Brandon grabbed a drummy off Monique's tray. "Here, take this. It's my good deed for the day. Feeding the hungry." And he threw the chicken wing at me. It hit me in the chest, the grease instantly staining my T-shirt, and if my insides really were black, at that moment they were definitely turning red.

Red and Dre looked at me, both their mouths open in disbelief. I could tell they could see the anger in my face, in my eyes. Dre slid down, and Red got up from the table, moved away from us. I brushed the over-fried wing off my lap, opened my milk carton, took a swig, and then, with all my might, beamed the container at Brandon's head. He moved just in time and the open milk box smashed into the table behind him. Brown liquid exploded everywhere, and everyone at that table whipped around to see what was happening. Brandon sprang from his seat, but before he could even make a move I had picked up my plastic tray and whacked him over the head. He fell backward, and I kept coming. I dove across the table and after that, it was just like it was when I was sprinting. I didn't hear nothing. Not even Monique squealing. And I didn't feel nothing either. I just lifted my arms, fists tight, and lowered them like hammers down onto Brandon's face. I had been good. So good. Altercation free. For seventeen hours and two freakin' minutes.

The third, fourth, and fifth minute of the seventeenth hour were the altercation minutes. But the sixth was the longest minute of them all – the embarrassing walk to the principal's office.

"You want to tell me what happened, or should I tell you?" Principal Marshall closed his door behind him and took a seat at his desk. Arms folded across his chest, he waited for me to answer. But I didn't. I just slouched in the chair and stared into my lap, biting on my bottom lip, trying to turn the red inside back to black. I was just so mad, and I couldn't get it to go away. Mr Perham, or as everyone called him, Big Perm, because of his last name and because he had bone-straight permed hair, is who pulled me off Brandon. He yoked me up in some kind of full nelson armlock and practically dragged me to a hard to do when you're desperately trying to explain yourself. "About how my mother works in a cafeteria, and about my neighbourhood, and all that. He always trying me, and he don't even know me like that. Just wouldn't shut up."

Marshall leaned back in his seat. "So instead of telling a teacher, you jumped on him?"

Well, yeah. Brandon needed a beat-down as far as I was concerned. Somebody had to do it, and well, this wasn't the first time I had been in this kind of an "altercation." I mean, there was the time I yelled at Mr Crue, because he kept being mean about us not understanding Spanish well enough to speak in the perfect accent or whatever. He was just riding us too hard for not rolling our *r's,* and one day I just lost it. After class everybody told me he deserved it, but I still caught a detention for it. And then another time Damon "DW" Woods told everybody that I kissed this girl named Janine, who was the only pretty girl who liked me, but I hadn't, and I hadn't told DW that lie. I just told him that me and Janine exchanged phone numbers. Once she found out, Janine said I was disgusting and stopped talking to me. So I punched Damon in the stomach. He cried and ran to Marshall and I got suspended for that one, and then Janine liked me again. But I was already over her. And me and Brandon had a bunch of other moments, but it was mostly just a lot of yelling – really just me yelling and him laughing, but not no more. No more getting the Brandon runaround. Then it hit me – run . . . around. Running. The team! Coach made a deal with my mother. I only had one shot. No mess-ups, no do-overs, no . . . altercations! But what was I supposed to do?

"What would *you* have done?" I asked Mr Marshall. The tears were teetering in and out, in and out, and I was trying my best to keep them in. "You never been pushed before, to the point you just couldn't take it?"

Principal Marshall cocked his head to the side and studied me. Then he hunched forward again and put his face in his palms, as if he was remembering a time he went through this. Then he wiped his hands down his face like he was washing that memory away.

"I'm going to deal with Brandon, but you . . . ," he said, his voice now a little softer, "you gotta get it together, Castle. I know you've been through some things, but you just can't keep doing this." He stood up from his desk and came around to the front. "I'm not going to give you a full suspension this time, but you do have to go home for the rest of the day." He reached behind him for the big black telephone. "Here." He held the phone toward me. "Call your mum."

Now, I knew that Principal Marshall was letting me off the hook, big-time, but there was no way I could call my mother and tell her that I needed her to come get me from school. No way. I hadn't even really been *on* the running team and I was already about to be kicked off. I hadn't even been to a practise yet! Plus what was I gonna say? That I punched a jerk for talking trash about me? I mean, that is what happened, and as awesome as that sounds, my mother would've hit me with the "How many times do I have to tell you to be the bigger person!" followed by some crazy punishment that involved me coming to the hospital with her, which was always wack.

"I can't," I shot back at the principal.

"You can't what?"

"I can't call her."

He looked confused. "And why not?"

"I don't know," I said, trying to think of a good reason. A good lie. But nothing came. "I just can't." Then it hit me. "But I can call my uncle."

"Your uncle," he said matter-of-factly, like he knew that was impossible. The other thing I should tell you about files is that sometimes they have way too much information about you in them. Stuff that don't be nobody's business. "And where is this uncle?"

"He's working, but he can come get me."

"Why haven't I ever heard of this uncle before?" he asked suspiciously.

"He's been gone," I explained, trying to keep a straight face. Looked him dead in the eye. "But he's back now." Yikes. Not really that smooth of an answer.

Mr Marshall just sat there squinting at me, one eye slightly more closed than the other, tapping his leg. Then he humphed and handed me the phone.

"Call him." He sighed.

I unzipped my backpack and dug around for the card that said THE DEFENDERS, COACH, in black block letters. I dialed and waited while it rang. *Come on, come on, pick it up,* I thought. *Please, pick it up.*

"Yes." It was Coach's voice on the other end of the phone, but he didn't say hello or nothing so it caught me off guard.

"Hello?" I said.

"Who's this?"

"It's me, Castle, um, uh . . . ," I spoke low into the phone. "Ghost."

"Ghost? Boy, what are you doing calling me at" – he paused, I guess to check the time –"at twelve twenty-two? Aren't you in school?"

"Yeah, but I need you to come get me," I said, looking up at Principal Marshall, who was staring a hole in my head. I was trying not to say "uncle," which was what he was waiting for. "I got in trouble."

"What?" Coach said, and before I could say anything else, he told me to hold on. "Nine seventy-five, ma'am. Uh-huh. Thank you so much. Have a good day." Then the sound of a door slamming. "Now, what you talking about, Ghost?"

"I got in trouble and they're suspending me for the day, so I need you to come get me."

"Why you calling me? Why don't you call your . . ." and before he could even finish his sentence, he answered his own question. "Oh. I see. Kid, you're already killing me."

I glanced up at Principal Marshall again. He was getting antsy, and I knew I only had a few seconds before he snatched the phone. Turns out I had even less than a few seconds.

"Give me the phone," Principal Marshall said, getting up and grabbing it from me. Then he aired everything out. "Hello, Principal Marshall here. Is this Castle's uncle?"

I dropped my head and waited to pretty much be body slammed.

"Uh-huh. Yes. Well, I need him off the premises as soon as possible. Just for the rest of the day." Principal Marshall sat on the edge of his desk, waiting for me to look him in the eye. But I wouldn't. I just looked around the office at all the posters that said stuff like EXCELLENCE and DISCIPLINE. And he had pictures of past students, probably kids who did excellent things. Disciplined things. Holding ribbons at a science fair. Clutching a trophy. Some kid giving the camera a thumbs-up like a cornball. Probably all good students, not kids like me. Mr Marshall was uh-huh-ing Coach. "Uh-huh. I see. Okay."

Then he handed the phone back to me, but Coach had already hung up. Principal Marshall walked back behind his desk and took a seat.

"What did he say?" I asked, bracing for the slam.

"He said he'll be here in a minute." It would've been the worst mistake ever to smile, but I sure wanted to.

I sat there in the office while the principal went on about his business, flipping through folders, clicking at something on his computer, scribbling in a notepad, when I finally asked him about the pictures of the different students on the wall.

"Who those kids?" I asked, biting a fingernail. Must've snagged it in the scuffle.

Principal Marshall looked up from all his busywork.

"You don't get to ask me any questions until tomorrow," he snapped. His tone was sharp, and I could tell he wasn't playing. "I don't want to hear your voice. Your job right now is to sit there and wait for your uncle. Got it?"

I just nodded and sank into myself. Thankfully, it wasn't too long before Coach came marching up the hallway. The look he gave me was just as bad as the look Mr Marshall had given me, which were like the looks my mum gave me whenever I was in these situations. The *I'm so disappointed in you* look, which is way worse than the I'm *mad* look.

"I'm here to get Castle," Coach said to the secretary, Mrs. Dickson.

"Okay, just sign him out," she said.

Coach scribbled something on a piece of paper, checked his watch, jotted the time down, met the principal, shook his hand, apologised to him for what I did, and we were out of there. On the way down the hall, Coach didn't say a thing. Not a word. But as soon as we got in his cab, he lit me up.

"What were you thinking telling those people I'm your uncle? Do you know that's probably against the law? I'm not sure if it is or isn't but it probably is, and if it is, you got me out here committing crimes. I've known you for one day. One day! And I just kidnapped you!"

I kept quiet because Coach was really

mad. Plus, I was super grateful that he came and got me, and I didn't want to say anything to mess that up. Shoot, he might've turned around and took me back to the school if I said the wrong thing.

Then finally, after a few minutes, he calmed down a little and asked, "What happened anyway?"

"I got in a fight." I stared out the window as we passed Mr Charles's store.

"Care to elaborate?" Coach pried.

"Okay. So there's this guy, Brandon Simmons. He's always getting on me about my mum and where I live and how I look and all that. And today, I just couldn't take it no more." I faced Coach. He glanced at me and then back to the road. "So I jumped on him. Beat him down."

"And what, you think that makes you tough?"Coach scoffed.

I thought about it for a second. "I don't know."

"Does that make it right?" he asked.

What is it about adults that makes them all just say the same things? Like they all studied the same book about grown-up-ness, memorizing phrases like, *Does that make it right?* and *Be the bigger person.*

I just shrugged. Spoke with my shoulders. I kinda wanted to say, *Yes. Yes, me punching Brandon in the face makes it right, because he had been begging for it for forever.* It made it right for everybody he joked on, and those kids would've given me their honour roll certificates for what I did. That wasn't the answer Coach was looking for. But man, that's how I felt.

Coach drove through town, and eventually we ended up at Martin Luther King Park. He said that since I had cost him a half day's worth of fares – the front seat wasn't even all junky yet – I would have to make it up to him by putting in extra work at the track, which was fine with me.

Coach grabbed his whistle and clipboard from the glove compartment. "Okay, here's how you're spending your suspension. We got us three hours before practise. We're going to use this time to get you caught up on the way all this goes."

"How all what goes?"

"Being on my team, boy."

I could tell he was still irritated, but not as much as he had been.

We headed over to the track, the bright white lines marking out the red lanes, the green field in the middle.

"Okay, so first things first. Where's your practise clothes?" Coach asked.

"These them," I said.

"You have on jeans and high-tops," he stated the obvious.

I looked at myself. There was a stain on my trainers. A new one. Maybe ketchup. Or chocolate milk. "So?" I said. "What's wrong with that?"

Coach sat down on a bench, stretched his legs out. "You know what, don't worry about it. We'll figure that out later. Let's just start with some stretching."

Apparently there were a whole slew of different kinds of stretches, and Coach showed me how to do them all. Each one was for a different reason. This one for this part of the leg, that one for that part of the leg, another one for your back. Then jumping jacks, toe touches, push-ups. It all seemed silly to me, but not as silly as the next part – the two-lap warm-up jog.

Me and Coach bounced around the track, him telling me to keep my arms tucked, which was actually hard to do. He said form is everything when it comes to running, and that it has more to do with form than how fast your legs move. That didn't sound right. To me, it seemed like if my arms were tucked but my legs weren't moving fast, then I wasn't gonna be beating nobody. Just common sense. But then again, I didn't think a two-lap jog – as slow as we were jogging – would get me going, but by the time we finished I was pouring sweat.

"Good, good," he said as we got back to the bench. He bounced around on his toes like a boxer before finally settling down. "Feels good, don't it?"

I wiped my face with my shirt and took a seat. I was tired and energized at the same time, which was weird.

"I didn't do it to make me feel tough," I blurted out of nowhere.

Coach stopped bouncing. He sat down next to me and grabbed a towel from his bag.

"What you talking about?" he asked,

wiping sweat from his bald head. More like buffing it off.

"What you asked me in the car? If beating up Brandon makes me tough," I reminded him. "I said I didn't know, but I do." We locked eyes. "The answer is no, it don't make me tough."

Coach moved the towel from his head to his neck. "So what does it make you, then?"

"I don't know, but not tough." I thought for a second. "Because for something to make you feel tough, you gotta be a little bit scared of it at first. Then you gotta beat it. But I wasn't scared of Brandon at all. He's just a big guy with a big mouth. That isn't really all that scary to me." I had been thinking about this when we were running around the track, warming up. In between Coach's tips about form and all that stuff, my brain was kicking that question around.

"Let me guess," Coach said, now flinging the towel over his shoulder. "You're one of these kids who isn't scared of nothing or nobody."

"Nah." I chuckled just for a second because I knew the kinds of kids Coach was talking about. The kids who say they ain't scared but really be scared of everything. Kids like Brandon. He talked all that trash and teased people because he was shook. A cupcake. But that wasn't me.

"I'm not saying that. I've definitely been scared of somebody before. Real scared," I added, thinking about how loud a gun sounds when it's fired in a small room. "That's how come I know how to run so fast. But now, the only person I'm scared of, other than my mother . . . I mean, like, I do things I know aren't cool, but even though I know they aren't cool, like beating on Brandon, all of a sudden I'm doing it anyway, y'know? So I guess . . . I guess the only other person I'm really scared of, maybe . . . is me."

A grunt seeped from Coach. He rubbed his right knee.

"I hear ya, kid," he said, wincing, stretching out his right leg, bending it, then straightening it. Then he did the same to the left. "Trouble is, you can't run away from yourself." Coach snatched the towel from his shoulder, folded into a perfect square, and set it in the space between us. "Unfortunately," he said, "isn't *nobody* that fast."

4

WORLD RECORD FOR THE WORST DAY EVER

I KNOW IT seems like this was the best suspension day maybe in history. And to be honest, it was. At least, at first. I got to punch that jerk Brandon in the face – I know, I know, not cool, but still! – leave school early, and hang out at the track with my new coach – because I was on a team now – who turned out to be a pretty cool dude. Me and Coach didn't go no further into my life or nothing like that, which was a good thing because I never really told nobody about my dad. Instead Coach asked me who my favourite basketball player was.

"LeBron," I said, like it should've been obvious. "Who else?"

"Who else?" Coach said, surprised. "Uh . . . let me think . . . Michael Jordan?"

"Jordan? Come on, man. Jordan is like somebody's granddaddy. Jordan don't wanna see LeBron on his worst day. LeBron could be sick from a bad batch of cafeteria chicken drummies and still give Jordan the business."

Coach stood up. "See, that's the problem with you kids. Y'all don't know what a true *champ* is."

"Coach, I hate to break it to you, but LeBron is a champ. He got *rangs*," I said, holding up two fingers and wiggling them around.

"But Jordan has *six*." Now Coach held up both his hands. All five fingers spread on his right, just his pointer finger up on his left. He wiggled them like I did. "Six!"

"Jordan got *six*?" Whoa! I probably should've known that, but I didn't. Dang. I knew he won a few, but six? "Is that the Guinness World Record?"

"The what?" Coach asked.

"The Guinness World Record. Gotta be." I put it in my head to check the book when I got a chance.

"I don't know, probably. He was the greatest of all time." Coach shot an invisible jump shot, his tongue hanging out his mouth. It looked ridiculous. Clearly he wasn't a ballplayer.

Then I asked him about that guy I read about who was supposed to be the fastest man alive. Usain Bolt. Coach knew all about him, too.

"Usain ran a nine-five-eight," Coach said.

"What's that mean?" I asked, because the numbers nine, five, and eight meant nothing to me. They're not points or nothing like that. At least I didn't think they were. I actually wasn't even really sure if you could score points in track or not. Just seemed like the kind of sport you just win ribbons and medals or whatever.

"That was his time for the one hundred metre." Coach pointed up the track toward the start line he had had everybody sprinting from the day before. "From there" – he moved his hand to the finish line – "to there. Nine seconds and fifty-eight milliseconds. The boy is like lightning."

I looked at the distance and in my head counted, one Mississippi, two Mississippi, three Mississippi, and pictured myself running. Nine seconds seemed like a pretty long time.

"But that ain't even that fast," I said. Plus

it just didn't seem like one hundred metres was all that long. I mean, I had just run it the day before in what had to be six or seven seconds. Couldn't have been more than eight.

"You don't think so?" Coach asked, flashing a sly grin. "You think you can beat that?"

I looked at the distance again. One Mississippi, two Mississippi . . . "I don't know." I shrugged. "Probably."

This was when the best day ever went bad. Coach told me to try to run one hundred metres in nine seconds and fifty-eight milliseconds – Bolt's time. He stood at the finish line with his whistle in his mouth. I rolled my pants up to my knees and my shirtsleeves up to my shoulders just like I had done the day before.

"On my whistle," Coach said, holding up the stopwatch. "On your mark, get set," and then, *badeep!* I took off down the track running as fast as I could, legs pumping, arms pumping, heart pumping, until I got to the finish line.

"Ohhhh," Coach howled excitedly. I felt good. Knew that I had proven my point. I bopped over to Coach with my hand up, ready for the high five. But Coach never lifted his hand.

"Not even close!" he yelped. "Not. Even. Freakin'. Close. You ran a twelve-five." And before I could even respond, he barked, "Back on the line!"

I jogged back to the start. Coach blew the whistle. I ran. He blew the whistle. I ran. Again, and again, and again. Each time I came in a little slower than the last. My head started swimming, my chest burning, and my legs got all gooey, like all the running was turning my bones to liquid or something.

After the fifth try, Coach yelled out, "Fourteen seconds? *Fourteen seconds*? On the track, that might as well be fourteen minutes! Are you kidding me?"

I bent over and planted my hands on my knees. My legs were shaking, but only on the inside. Like my muscles were . . . shivering. My heart was pounding as fast as my feet had pounded the track. Maybe even faster. My stomach was flipping, and I just knew that my fries were gonna come out as mashed potatoes all over the place. Coach walked over, his shadow making the red track burgundy around me. He leaned in and said lightly, almost as if he were whispering to me, "Back on the line."

That's when I lost it.

"What . . . what? What . . . again? I . . . need . . . a break," I panted. "I'm tired."

"Tired?" Coach squealed, and I could hear the smile in his voice. I glanced up and there it was, big and chipped and wide like whatever words were hiding behind those teeth, he was struggling to keep in. So he let them out. "You know who's *really* tired, son? Your principal." Coach put his hands up, palms facing me as if to stop me from even thinking about responding. Then he continued, "No, no. You know who's really, *really* tired? Your mother. She's *so* tired. *So* tired. And she's gonna be even more exhausted when she hears about your suspension."

"Come on, Coach," I begged. "That's messed up."

"Come on, nothing," Coach said like every old black person says when they don't have a good comeback. He grabbed my shoulder and stood me straight. "Bending over cuts off your air," he said. "We stand straight up at all times. Understand?"

I nodded, now understanding what was

happening. I was being punished after all. This was Coach's way of telling me that I better stop acting up in school. If this was what the consequences of getting sent to Mr Marshall's office were going to be every time, I'd rather have him just call my mother.

"Now, Mr Better Than Bolt, get back on the line."

Coach made me do the sprint two or three more times before finally letting up, and the only reason I think he let me stop was because my sprint had broken down into that weird, sloppy trot the tall skinny kid, Sunny, had done at the practise the previous day. My shirt was gone. I had peeled it off and thrown it on the field just in case the wet cotton was weighing me down or something. My legs had pretty much clocked out, but instead of letting me just sit down and rest, Coach told me to walk it off.

"Walk it off?" I asked, annoyed and confused and almost ready to cry.

"Yeah, just walk around the track. It'll cool your body down slowly."

But I didn't want my body to cool down slowly. I wanted it to cool down immediately! So, yeah, at this point I had pretty much made up my mind that running was the dumbest sport ever. I mean you gotta move to warm up, and move to cool down? Don't make no sense. Cooldown should be, I don't know, some juice and an ice-pop or something like that. Not no walk.

Once I finished the first lap, Coach told me to take one more, and about halfway around the second lap of me mumbling under my breath about how stupid all this was, I could see the other runners – my new teammates – showing up, dropping their sports bags and water bottles and all that on the track, some of their parents trailing behind.

"This is gonna be it," Coach was preaching to everyone as I finally made it back to the other side of the track for the second time. "Ten girls, ten boys. Just so we're clear, this doesn't mean you still can't be cut. It just means you're not cut yet. Now, I'd like to keep it this way, but that's totally up to you. Got that?"

Everybody nodded, including a woman with braids who looked too old to be on the team even though she was dressed in running clothes. I had first noticed her from the other side of the track and figured she was somebody's mother . . . until she didn't sit down with the rest of the corny kids' cheering squad.

Coach went on about how this was the third day of practise for the spring season, and how he wanted to make sure we all knew each other, or at least make sure all the vets knew the newbies. I was still standing back, sort of outside the circle, as Coach started rattling off everybody's name.

"On the girls' side, for the vets we have Myisha Cherry, Brit-Brat Williams, Melissa Jordan, Dee Dee Gross, Krystal Speed . . ." Any girl with the last name Speed had to be fast. Kinda like any dude with the last name Bolt. Coach continued, "Deja Bullock, Lynn Tate, Kondra Fulmer, Nicky McNair." He paused and motioned toward the last girl. "And our newbie for the girls, Patina – but she told me a few minutes ago that she goes by Patty—Jones." Everybody clapped. "Patty, I got high hopes for you, young lady. Let's make it happen."

Then he started calling out the boys' names. First, the vets. "Eric Daye, Curron

Outlaw, Aaron Holmes, Mikey Farrar, Freddy Hayes, Josh 'J.J.' Jerome, and Chris Myers. You boys better look out for our newbies, Lu Richardson, Sunny Lancaster . . ." And this was when Coach turned to me. "And as of yesterday, this kid. Castle Cran—"

"Ghost," I cut him off before he could even get the *shaw* out. "Just call me Ghost."

Coach gave me a look. Actually, everybody gave me a look. Probably because I didn't have no shirt on, and my pants were rolled to my knees, and my belt was pulled so tight that it made the denim bunch around my waist like genie pants. But whatever.

"I was gonna tell them that, son," Coach said. Then he turned back to the rest of the team. "Lastly, this is your assistant coach, Coach Whit." Coach Whit was the woman with the braids. She also had chubby cheeks, and like I said, she looked too old to be on the team, but she definitely didn't look old enough to be nobody's coach. Then she pulled a whistle from underneath her sweatshirt, so that pretty much meant she was.

"Give it up for your squad," Coach told us,

slapping his hands together. "This is gonna be a great season!" Everybody cheered and clapped for maybe ten seconds before Coach shut it down and told us it was time to get to work.

He divided everyone up into whatever their speciality was. Because most of the other kids had been running track for, like, forever, Coach knew who was a sprinter, who ran long stuff, and who ran all the junk in the middle. As far as the newbies were concerned, Sunny was a long runner and Patty ran the in-between. Me and Lu were the sprinters. (I never even knew I was a sprinter!) So guess what we were doing for practise? Sprinting. And guess who had just finished sprinting and didn't get to take a break? Me.

"Today is Wednesday, and Mikey, why don't you inform our newbies about what sprinters do on Wednesdays," Coach said. Mikey was a vet sprinter. A light-skinned kid with braces and a rock face. The kind of guy who you didn't really say too much to, because you just assumed he wouldn't say nothing back. Except to Coach, of course.

"Ladders," Mikey grumbled.

"That's right." Coach paced back and forth. "Four, three, two, one, one, two, three, four." Every time Coach called a number, he clapped his hands together like a cheerleader.

Okay. Let me explain what Coach was talking about, because I didn't have a clue at first either. All those numbers, the fours and the threes and all that, yeah, add a "hundred" on the end, and then add a "metres" on the end of that. So four hundred metres, three hundred metres, two hundred metres, and so on. We had to run those. Down the ladder to one hundred, then back up to four. I didn't think the day that started kind of bad, then got good, then got bad, then got better, then got bad again, could get worse until Coach told me, Lu, Mikey, and Aaron – the four sprinters on the boys' side – to get on the line, four words I was already sick and tired of hearing.

The whistle blew, and . . . well . . . Lu, Mikey, and Aaron blew me away.

Back on the line, this time for the three hundred. Toasted.

Back on the line, now, the two hundred. Roasted.

Back on the line for the one hundred. Dusted.

"Five-minute break," Coach said. "Grab some water." He came over to me, put his hand on my shoulder. I was literally folded in half, trying to catch my breath. My eyes were watering, but I knew better than to cry. I'm no crybaby. Especially not over no running.

"You all right?" Coach asked. I couldn't get the words out. Every time I tried to speak, the sound was shoved back in my throat by a sharp inhale. So I just nodded. Then Coach squeezed my shoulder and pulled me up so that I was standing straight. "Remember what I told you. Stand tall." I put my hands on my head, wove my fingers together. "Now hustle up and get some water." Coach nudged me. "You only got three minutes."

Here's the other thing that I didn't really know about being on a team. There are rules to drinking water. I mean, I guess it might be different on different kinds of teams, but on this team, everybody had their own water bottle that they had brought with them. So when I went over to the bench with the other sprinters, I just sat down. Didn't ask nobody for a swig or nothing because . . . I don't know . . . it just didn't seem like something I should do. The only feel I had for these guys was that Lu was cocky, and Mikey seemed way too serious to share, and Aaron . . . well, I couldn't get a read on him at all yet. So I figured, three minutes to catch my breath was just as good as water. It would have to be.

"Where's your water, newbie?" Aaron asked, looking down the row.

"I . . . forgot it . . . ," I replied, the fire in my chest finally cooling down.

"Here." Aaron held his bottle out. "Take some. And don't put your mouth on it either."

Lu leaned back so I could grab Aaron's bottle. I held it above my head and squeezed the bottle until the water shot through the nozzle like a jet stream, splashing me in the face, some even getting in my nose. Eventually I hit the target – my mouth, which was when I realised I was wrong. Water was *way* better than just catching your breath. Way, way better. After I handed the bottle back to Aaron, Lu finally had something to say.

"Yo, what you doing here?" he asked. The way he said it made it seem like the words had been bubbling up inside him.

"What you mean?" I replied. "I'm doing the same thing you doing. Running."

Lu looked at me like I was speaking a different language. "Is that what you call that?" he jabbed. "I mean, yesterday you were big and bad, and today you just . . . bad. Plus, we all had to try out to prove we belong here, and you just walk on our track like you one of us?" Lu was giving me a stink-eyed stare, and I was looking to see if Aaron or Mikey agreed with him, but neither of them showed any sign of hate. I got the feeling Mikey never showed any sign of anything. Ever. Guy was a blank slate.

I tried to keep my cool, because I was all the way clear on what the punishment would be if I did something stupid. Plus, he was just talking trash. And it was just a little bit of trash. He wasn't gonna do nothing to me. I knew that for sure.

Still, I had to ask, "You mad about

yesterday? Is that what this is about? Me proving that you're not all that fast?" Then I had to add, "That you just got on a fancy suit, trying to front like you Usain Bolt." It felt good to throw that name out there like I really knew what I was talking about, especially since I had to pretend like I didn't think Lu's gear was the sweetest I had ever seen. Especially the shoes. Oh man, those shoes. They were bright green and looked like they were specially made just for him. They *had* to have been helping him run.

"Nobody trying to be Bolt. I'm gonna be better than Bolt. Plus, at least I got on running clothes. You out here in your daddy's gear pretending to be something you not."

Oh no. I could feel the altercation-ness creeping up in my chest like a new kind of lightning. The black was turning red again, and I really wasn't trying to be a repeat offender of the bully beat-down. Not in the same day. But Lu was begging for it.

"What you say about my daddy?" I asked, my head cocked to the side, which is pretty much the universal symbol for *watch yourself, homie.*

"I'm just saying if you can't afford running gear, at least wear pants that fit. And what are those shoes? *Sikes*? *Freeboks*?"

"Chill," Mikey said, flat. That's all he said. Just, "Chill."

Aaron followed up. "Yeah, take it out on the track, newbies."

Luckily, Coach blew the whistle and called us all back to the starting line. I stood up. Lu stood up. We eyeballed each other for a second until Coach barked, "Hustle up!" Aaron finally pushed me toward the track, and Lu had no clue how lucky he was.

It was time to run back up the "ladder." Starting with the one hundred. My adrenaline was still pumping from all that trash Lu was talking. I didn't even do nothing to this dude, and he just felt like he could snap on me. Like I was some chump. *Who is he?* I thought. What gave him the right to just make fun of me for no reason? Like he was perfect. *He's* the one God didn't colour in. *He's* the one who looked weird. Why didn't I at least get him on that? Stupid. But that's okay, because when Coach blew the whistle, I kept up with Lu on the one hundred.

Matter fact, I might've even beat him. On the two, I did okay. But it was on the three where the day got *even* worse.

I was wiped, but there was nothing that was going to make me quit. Not after all that trash talk. Plus, I could tell Lu was tired too. He was panting even harder than I was, and he didn't even have the pre-workout workout! Coach even had to tell him to stop bending over, which made me feel good, to know I wasn't the only one who felt like I was dying. But when the whistle blew, and we started running, what I didn't know was that one of my shoes had come untied. By the time I realised one lace was flapping around, we were halfway through the sprint, and I was still keeping up with Lu and there was nothing that was going to stop me from beating him. So I pushed on. We rounded the bend, Lu leaning into it, which I honestly thought was kind of cool, and then we hit the straightaway. I had my elbows tucked and everything. But . . . my shoelaces. They apparently hated me. I stepped on one, I guess. I mean, who really knows how anyone trips over shoelaces. They're just laces. How can you trip over a lace? I don't know, but I did. And it was bad. Not only did I do the whole slow-motion, stumble – stumble –stumble – fall thing, but to make it *even* worse (yeah, we're in like negative worse at this point), my shoes came off. Both! *Off!*

Of course, you know that at the exact moment I slammed into the track, everybody else – who had all been off working on their specialties – just happened to be looking toward us.

Ohhhhhhh! was literally what everyone howled. Everyone. Even Coach. I lay there on my stomach for a second, before finally rolling over and sitting up.

"You okay?" Coach said, jogging over. I looked behind me. Lu was just finishing the sprint and was now staring back down the straightaway. I looked at my hands and knees. They were black and white with track burn. "Come on." Coach grabbed me by the arm and helped me up. "Walk it off."

But walking it off had a whole other meaning for me this time. It meant walking, in my dirty, soggy socks, down the track to get my trainers, which might've been more embarrassing than any joke anyone has ever cracked on me. And walking it off also meant actually walking it off. As in, walking it off the track.

"Just sit this last one out, son," Coach said, before turning back toward the other sprinters all cracking up. Even Mikey. And especially Lu. "That's enough laughing. On the line!" Coach barked, lifting the whistle back to his lips.

After practise, everybody gathered around the bench, grabbed their bags, and headed off to meet their parents. I sat with my head in my lap, waiting for everyone to disappear. Or waiting for myself to. I'd rolled my jeans down – crinkled from knee to ankle – and I had put my wet shirt back on.

"Scoot over, dude," a girl voice said. I lifted my head, and there was Patty. She sat down next to me and started unlacing her shoes, which by the way, were also pretty dope. I looked straight ahead, out at the track, those stupid white lines teasing me like everybody else. "Don't worry about today," Patty said sweetly. "You're not the first person to crash out like that." She eased her heels out of her shoes. "And you won't be the last."

I glanced over at Coach, who was standing off to the side talking to Sunny and the man standing next to Sunny, who I figured was his father. He looked like a businessman. Grey suit. Tie. Beard. Glasses. The whole getup.

"I just wanted to beat him, to shut him up." I kept my eye on those white lines. I didn't want Patty to see whatever might've been showing on my face.

"Who, Lu?" she asked, her voice brightening up, happy like this was some kind of joke. "Don't pay that fool no mind. He just mad he albino."

Now I turned to Patty, because I didn't have a clue what she was talking about. Albino? Was that some kind of sickness? Was he infected with something? Or was it like he was in special ed, because if that was what albino meant, then people probably thought I was albino too.

"Albino?" I repeated.

"Yeah," she replied. She must have sensed I was clueless, because she continued, "Wait.

You don't know what albino is?"

I shook my head. Then Patty shook hers.

"So, it's basically when you born without the brownness in your skin," she explained. "That lady who be cheering for him all crazy at practise, that's his mother."

The woman was my complexion. Medium brown.

"And his daddy dark-skinned. So no way he could just come out white. Feel me? That's albino."

Somebody called out for Patty, a small voice. A little girl came running toward us. "So yeah, Ghost – Ghost, right?" Patty said, standing up.

"Yeah."

"That's why Lu acts like that. Trust me, I know. I used to go to school with him. He was picked on crazy until he started running. Matter fact, kids used to call *him* Ghost," Patty explained. The little girl had finally reached us. She threw her arms around Patty and squeezed tight.

"Ghost, this my baby sister, Madison."

Madison looked at me. "Hey, Madison,"

I said. She did a weird wave. Just jabbed her arm up and snapped it down real quick. Then she buried her face in Patty's stomach. She was probably freaked out by my name.

"Okay, okay, let's go," Patty said, looking over at a white woman. "Mumly's waiting for us." Then she looked at me and said, "And before you start wondering if I'm reversed albino or something, me and Madison are adopted. So no need to be weird about it, 'kay?"

"Oh, I wasn't . . . I . . . " I stammered, trying to pretend like the whole reversed albino thing didn't pop right up in my head the second she called that white lady "Mumly," which was obviously one of those mum nicknames, like . . . I don't know . . . "Ma" or something.

"It's cool," Patty said, smiling. She picked up her bag and threw it over her shoulder. Then she bent down and lifted her sister, holding her tight to her hip, and they left. Once Patty hobbled past Coach, Sunny and his dad started walking with her. Sunny turned around awkwardly and threw his hand up in the air to me.

"Good job today, Ghost!" he yelled, and

even though I would normally think this was some kind of slick way of making fun of me, the look on Sunny's face and the way his voice sounded made me think that he really meant it. So I waved back and said, nowhere near loud enough for him to actually hear me, "Thanks."

That left me and Coach. When we got to his cab, I threw my backpack on the floor in the back, slammed the door, and lay down on the sticky leather.

"If you sit back there, I gotta treat you like a customer, kid," Coach said, starting the car. I didn't say anything. Coach turned around in his seat and glared at me. "Okay, then fine. I'm gonna run the metre. If you gonna make me drive you home in silence, I might as well get paid for it."

Still, nothing from me. Not a word. Nothing to say. All I could think about was how stupid it felt to crash and burn on the track like that on my first real day of practise, and how Brandon Simmons would've laughed me off the planet if he was there to see that, and how I had finally beaten him up for talking smack about me and would've done it again, and how Patty said

Lu had (was?) albino, and how she had a white mother, and ladders were the worst, four-three-two-one-one-two-three-four, and water bottles, and how come I didn't know any of this, and how come everybody's shoes were so good, especially Lu's and Patty's. And probably Usain Bolt's.

". . . I swear, I almost broke my nose, kid. I mean, I just clipped the hurdle and dove face-first to the ground." Despite his riding-in-silence comment, Coach was blathering on, probably telling me a story, but I wasn't really listening. He continued, "So I know what it's like to be embarrassed in front of your teammates. Trust me, tomorrow nobody will even remember."

I heard that part, that tomorrow nobody would remember, and I'm not sure if I believed it or not, but I knew what I could do to help the situation. In addition to the ladders, water bottles, white parents, albino thinking, I also thought myself up a plan.

When we pulled up in front of my house, Coach put the car in park.

"Twenty dollars," he said, trying to lighten the situation.

"Coach."

"Nah, nah, don't try to dash on me," he insisted. "You done already robbed me for half a day's pay."

"But I paid you back already with all that sprinting I gave you earlier," I groaned.

Coach did a double take. "Oh, you thought that was for *me?*" He pressed a finger to his chest.

I shook my head and unlocked the door. After I got out, Coach rolled down the window. The car slowly drifted forward. "Remember what I said, Ghost. . . ." He accelerated slightly. "Tomorrow it won't matter. It'll be a new day. A new chance!"

When I got inside my house, I didn't waste any time. I knew what I needed to do, and I knew that I had to do it before my mother got home and made me eat dinner and watch some sappy flick with her while she procrastinated doing *her* homework. See, besides working in a hospital cafeteria, she was also taking online classes (there were also textbooks in that big bag), trying to get her nursing degree. She always says she can't wait to one day trade that serving spoon for a stethoscope, and this house for a new one not in Glass Manor. But she hated homework. I guess I get that from her.

I dropped my bag on the couch and headed straight for the kitchen. The drawer next to the stove was where my mother kept leftover duck sauce, soy sauce, chopsticks, menus, tape, screwdrivers, but most importantly, all her vouchers, organized and paperclipped by product. Seemed like everybody was having a sale on ketchup, which was a good thing because ketchup always made cafeteria food taste better. Way better. Along with the vouchers (and all the other stuff) were the scissors she used to cut those coupons. These weren't just regular scissors, though. Nope. These were hospital scissors. At least that's where my mum got them from, and they were big, and shiny, and heavy, like if a doctor gotta cut somebody's arm off or something, he could just use these bad boys and . . . *snip, snip,* bye-bye arm. Which was why I knew they'd be perfect for what I needed them for.

I grabbed the scissors and sat down on the kitchen floor. Using one foot to press against the heel of the other, I pushed my trainers off. I yanked the laces out of both, so the floppy tongues fell forward like drawbridges coming down out of beat-up, leather, no-named fortresses. Because here's the truth – I was still so angry about what happened on the track. Embarrassed. There was so much noise inside of me. So much of everybody's laughing. So starting with the left shoe, I took those big scissors and began cutting and cutting, performing my own kind of surgery, the blades sawing and slicing into the black leather until the high parts of my high-tops were gone.

5

WORLD RECORD FOR THE MOST RUNAWAYS IN A SINGLE DAY

I WONDER IF doctors ever cut off somebody's arm or leg and afterward realise that they made a huge mistake. Like, totally blew it. Because that's definitely how I felt about low-topping my high-tops, but not until I got to school the next day.

I was cool with my new shoes when I first did it. Walked around the house totally hype about how much lighter they were, which would definitely help me out on the track. But when I heard my mum at the door, I took them off and, quickly, threw them in my room. I didn't really think she would notice that I cut my shoes in half, because she was usually so beat when she got home she never noticed anything but the couch. But still, I wanted to play it safe just in case she was in a bad mood and saw that I pretty much just threw half the money she paid for those trainers in the trash, buried under plastic to-go containers, all streaky and stinky with brown gravy and french dressing. She probably would've flipped out and, knowing her, would've made me get the glue and the needle and thread and the stapler and some tape and made me try to fix them, all while giving me the speech about "the value of a dollar." And that would've been even worse than her yelling at me or punishing me. Shoot, maybe even worse than ladders.

I was even still good with the shoes the next morning, which I was really happy about because a lot of times when you sleep on something, your sleep, for some reason, causes your mind to change. I don't know why, but it does. But when I woke up the next morning, wrapped in my blankets on the living room floor, I opened my bedroom door, peeked at my shoes as if they might have come to life in the middle of the night, and, thankfully, was still all right with them. Even after I got dressed and put them on, I wasn't too worried because my jeans came down long enough to cover the raggedy top and make them look regular.

What wasn't okay, though, were my legs. They felt like they had been cut off in my sleep, stuffed with dynamite and hot peppers, and then reattached. So even though my shoes were covered, I couldn't hide the fact that I was walking like a senior citizen zombie, which I feared would draw unnecessary attention – the last thing I needed.

When I got to school, first I looked around for Brandon Simmons. But he was nowhere to be found. The only reason I was checking for him was because he could always sniff out stuff like raggedy shoes, or whatever, not that he would've tried me two days in a row. If he did, he would've won because my legs were barely working, but he wouldn't test me, not after what had happened at lunch. If anything, people might've been teasing *him*. But like I said, he wasn't around. Principal Marshall was, though, and the first thing he said to me was that this had better be an altercation free day, followed by, "And Mr Simmons won't be joining us. He's suspended," which I have to say were the sweetest words I had heard in a while. I caught up with Dre in the hall for a few seconds.

He assumed I was limping because of the fight – battle wound – and was telling me how everyone was talking about how I mopped Brandon, even the people who got chocolate milk splashed on them.

"Bro, you like a hero," he said. "Like, you could run for class president right now and win, if you were into all that stuff." He threw his arm around me. "Picture that . . . President Cranshaw."

"Whatever, man." I slipped from under his arm, laughing to keep from wincing. I couldn't believe what I was hearing. Me, Ghost, a hero. Until social studies.

I wasn't really in the mood to learn about Alexander the Great, even though I did like the fact that he was called "the Great," but what I was even less in the mood for was sitting in front of Shamika Wilson. Shamika was . . . big. Like . . . huge. She had to be almost six feet tall in the seventh grade. And she had a birthmark that covered half her light-skinned face in dark brown, like a comic-book bad guy or something. But Shamika wasn't a mean girl. She was actually kinda cool. The only problem with her was that she was super silly, and she had a laugh as big as her body. But it was a real laugh. The kind that made her bend over. The kind that Coach was faking when I first met him. So when I sat down in front of her and bumped her desk, knocking one of her pencils on the floor, Shamika leaned over to pick it up, noticing my new and improved trainers. And then came the thunder. It just came out of nowhere, and once she starts laughing, Shamika can't stop. And the worst part is that she can sort of pass her laugh around the room to everybody, just because the sound of it is so outrageous. So if she laughs, everybody laughs. Imagine the sound a car makes when it's trying to start, but can't. Now, speed that sound up, and crank the volume high enough to blow out the windows in heaven. That's Shamika's laugh.

"What's so funny, Shamika?" Mr Hollow, the social studies teacher, asked, unamused. "Would you care to share it with the rest of the class?"

And that's pretty much when I started

to panic. When I had that doctor moment I was talking about when they cut somebody's arm off and then realise it was a bad idea – my shoes equalled that arm. And now Mr Hollow was basically asking to see my surgical screwup. Oh. No. Please, Shamika. Don't share it with the class. Don't share it with the class!

Shamika couldn't get herself together long enough to even speak, so instead she just pointed at my feet. And that was all it took for like sixty other eyeballs, including Mr Hollow's, to laser beam me and my trainers. I tried to cross my legs, then stick my feet further under the seat, then pull my jeans down, but then my butt was out. There was nowhere to hide, and the next few seconds, with the whole class howling, felt a gazillion times worse than Brandon's stupid jokes about my mum.

Mr Hollow finally shut it all down and went on about Alexander the Great, while I, Ghost the Worst, stared at the pages in my textbook, the stupid black words on the stupid white page all blurring together as solid black lines. I was literally shaking with embarrassment, like my insides had turned into ice. Ice that was cracking.

I wanted to break the desk.

Or flip it over.

Scream. Something. Anything.

Miraculously, the lunch bell rang. Everybody poured into the hallway, moving toward the cafeteria, some still talking about me, others playing and joking, slapping heads, jumping on backs, getting Mr Baskin, the school security guard, all mad as usual, forcing him to leave his post to deal with the craziness. And knowing that Baskin wasn't where he was supposed to be, once I *finally* got to the double doors of the lunchroom, a lunchroom I felt was waiting to eat *me*, I just kept walking – more like a sore walk-run – straight out the front door of the school.

I had never skipped class before. Never. I mean, I had my fair share of school problems, but I was never bold enough to just not go. And I definitely didn't have the guts to walk out in the middle of the day. But now I didn't have a choice. I had to get out of there.

Once I was outside, I broke out in a full-on run. I mean, I straight-up jetted, and because I was so scared of getting caught, I couldn't even feel the pain in my legs anymore. Adrenaline overload. I ran and ran, until I was far enough away from the school to not get caught. I turned down a busy street with a whole bunch of stores on it, just because it seemed like the easiest place to blend in. I *almost* went into a wig shop, just because I figured I might be able to grab a disguise. I mean, a wig would definitely do it. But . . . nah. Then there was the fish market. I looked in the window. Three short guys took huge fish – big like they were baby sharks or something – and hacked the heads off with giant knives. *WHAM!* That was wild, but somehow I could relate to the fish. Actually, I could kinda relate to the men chopping the heads off the fish, too. Then I came to a sporting goods store. That's when the best idea ever popped into my head.

"Welcome to Everything Sports," a lady greeted me at the door. Her name tag said TIA. She was wearing sweatpants and a basketball jersey with the store's name on the front. She didn't really look like she played sports, though.

Patty looked like an athlete, but this girl . . . not so much. I mean, she had on makeup and had her hair all done. "Let me know if you need some help finding anything," she said.

"Um," I hummed awkwardly. I tried not to look her directly in the face, just because I didn't want her to say nothing about me not being in school. Plus I felt weird about being the only person in the store. "Y'all got track stuff?" I asked. Then, trying to be more clear, I added, "Like, shoes?"

"Yep. Right over here," the girl, Tia, said, leading the way.

The track shoes at Everything Sports were amazing. Neon green and gold, shiny black and electric blue. They looked like they were full of power and speed, like just wearing them could get me closer to Usain Bolt's world record. They were just like Lu's.

I picked up one of the shoes, a silver one. Flipped it over to see the price. Then put it right back down. Yikes! Then I looked at a mean bright orange one, looked at the bottom.

"Want to try any of them?" Tia asked. She had been standing behind me the whole time.

I put the orange shoe back—they were even more! – and turned to face her. "Um . . . the silver ones, I guess."

"Size?" she asked.

"I don't really know, I think an eight? Maybe eight and a half." The truth is, I had no idea what size I wore. I couldn't remember. When me and Ma went to get my last pair, the ones I was wearing, the ones that now had their heads chopped off, the reason we went in the first place was because the trainers I had were too small. I think I was a seven then, and we had to bump up to an eight. But I just couldn't remember. Tia eyeballed my feet, and even though I knew she was trying to guess my shoe size, I couldn't help but think she was looking at my chewed-up dogs like, *What the*?

I was hearing Shamika's booming laugh ringing in my ears again when Tia finally chirped, "I'll bring a nine, too."

I took a seat on one of the benches and looked around at the boxing gloves and footballs and every other kind of sports equipment. There was a man working in the store too. He was standing next to a rack of skipping ropes, tossing a basketball back and forth from hand to hand, and occasionally spinning it on one finger, but only for like half a second. He probably wasn't no athlete either.

A few moments later Tia came back out with two boxes. "Okay," she said, setting the boxes down on the floor in front of me. "I got an eight and a nine, but no eight and a half." She popped the top of the first box. "Let's start with the nine."

She pulled the silver shoes from the box and set them down in front of me. I untied my frayed laces – I had to cut them, too – and slipped my trainers off, tucking them under the bench. Two more people walked into the store. Tia and the other guy greeted them; then Tia encouraged me to put the shoes on. "Walk around, jump up and down or whatever. Take your time and get a feel for them."

I put the shoes on. The nines fit perfectly. After I laced them tight, I stood up and bounced up and down a few times like Tia suggested. They felt amazing, almost like I didn't have any shoes on at all. I stepped in front of the mirror to check myself out. Man. It looked like I was wearing spaceships on my feet. Or silver bullets!

"How are they?" Tia came back over to check on me.

"They're good," I said, still staring at my feet in the mirror. I felt like they had some kind of power in them, and that power was pumping into me. The kind of power that shut down all laughter. I repeated, now looking at her, "They're good."

"Perfect." Tia nodded and went to talk to one of the other customers. And that's when I made my move.

At first I wasn't going to do it. I mean, when I went into the store, it was a thought, but only a thought. Not even like a real, *real* thought either, because I knew that I could just ask my mother to get them for me, and she would because she felt like this running thing was gonna keep me out of trouble. But when I saw how much they cost . . . I just couldn't ask her for them. I just couldn't. But these were "shut-up shoes." Nobody would have nothing to say about me with these on my feet. And that's when the thought became real.

I took the shoes off, and when Tia moved

to the other side of the store to show the baseball gloves to one of the people who had come in, and the other guy who worked there had run in the back to grab something for the other customer, I slipped the silver bullets in my backpack. I put the top back on the box and put the empty shoe box under the other one – the eights. Then I put my trainers back on as fast as I could. I slung my bag on my shoulder and headed for the door. Then, as I got there, Tia called out, "No good?"

I was stunned but shook it off and played it cool. "Um . . . they're amazing. I . . . I love them," I said, trying not to look her in the face. "Maybe I'll come back for them later." I pushed the door open. As soon as I stepped through the doorway, I took off.

I pounded down the street, waiting to hear someone yell, *Hey kid!* or *Thief! Somebody stop that kid!* Like they do on TV. But no one did. At least, I didn't hear none of that. The streets can be noisy with cars, and people bumbling around, not to mention when you're running scared, like I was, the only sound you really hear is the sound of your own heart banging like a scary soundtrack to the chase.

I turned the corner, still looking over my shoulder for the police, but I stopped running, because if a cop saw a random kid running down the street in the middle of a school day, might be a sign the kid's up to no good. And I was that kid, so I tried to throw off any potential cops by walking. But that felt cocky, so I did a weird *don't mind me, I'm just doing my old-lady power walk* thing. I knew it was only a matter of time before the police came out of nowhere, charging at me, ready to take me to jail all because I wanted some dope shoes to be a better runner . . . to be a better basketball player. Be better so nobody could say . . . anyway. The cops never came. I didn't stop, though. Too paranoid. I almost jumped into a trash can when a police car with his sirens on zipped past me. But he wasn't looking for me. Nope, he was looking for a *real* criminal. And I wasn't a *real* criminal. One with a *real* rap sheet.

Of course, after about five or six minutes of not quite running, not quite walking, I had to stop and figure out exactly where I was going. Didn't want to head home. I mean, I could've.

It would've been safe. But I just didn't want to go there. When I'm there by myself for too long, the house becomes some kind of time machine, teleporting me back three or four years, listening to my mum and dad fight and scream every night. Taking me back to all the bad stuff. So that was out. There was only one other place I thought was safe enough to go – Mr Charles's store.

When I got there, Mr Charles was talking to a deliveryman. He signed a piece of paper – one of those three-in-one papers – and a guy in dusty blue overalls ripped the pink one from the bottom and gave it to Mr Charles. Then the guy grabbed his metal carrier thing on wheels and rolled out.

"Castle?" Mr Charles said in his loud voice. He folded the pink piece of paper in half and tucked it somewhere behind the counter. He turned the TV down, then checked his watch, clearly confused about why I wasn't in school. But instead of just asking, he asked the usual. "Let me guess, sunflower seeds?" He snatched a bag off the wall. I wasn't even really thinking about sunflower seeds, but I did skip lunch, and since he brought it up . . .

"Let me guess, a dollar," I replied, as usual, digging into my pocket for a buck.

"Nope. Ten dollars," Mr Charles said, pulling the seeds back off the counter.

"Ten dollars?" I snipped. "What you mean, ten dollars?"

"I mean, sunflower seeds cost you ten bucks from now on, until you tell me why you're not in school." Mr Charles held his hand out, waiting for me to put the ten dollars I didn't have in it. Then he shrugged and put the sunflower seeds back up on the hook.

"Mr Charles," I moaned. "Are you serious?"

"Serious as a heart attack," he said, so predictably that I could've said it for him.

I looked at him for a second, y'know, trying to give him my best puppy-dog face even though I wasn't sure I even had one.

"Won't work," he said.

I leaned against the glass of the big fridge Mr Charles kept the deli meats in. "Okay," I huffed. "I left after social studies because kids were laughing at me."

Mr Charles came from behind the counter, propped himself up against the freezer. "Come again?"

"I said I left after social studies. Kids were laughing at me." This time louder.

"Laughing at what?"

I didn't say nothing. I just hiked my jeans up and let my shoes do the talking. Mr Charles looked down at my mangled kicks and dropped his mouth open.

"What'd you do?" he asked, stepping back to get a better view.

"I cut them," I said flat out, letting my pants drop back down.

"I can see that. But . . . why?"

I wanted to rip open my backpack and say, *To make them more like these!* But I didn't. Because then Mr Charles would've wanted to know where I got those dope kicks from and all that, and the next thing you know, he would've jacked the price of sunflower seeds up to a hundred bucks.

"I'm on a track team now. And they all got good shoes. Low-tops. And you can run better in low-tops."

"So you hacked half your trainers off?"

"Pretty much," I said, cool. "And today

at school, when some of the kids noticed, they laughed. So . . . I left. Please don't tell my mum." I'd been saying that a lot lately.

Mr Charles sighed, then went back behind the counter. He took the bag of seeds back off the hook and set them in front me.

"Okay. This one's on me," he said. But when I reached for them, Mr Charles wouldn't take his hand off the bag. "But no more running outta school. Especially just because people are laughing at you. People are always going to be laughing at you, Castle. Trust me."

"You been laughed at?" I asked. I was willing to bet that he never got made fun of. I mean, there was the whole *You look like a white James Brown* thing, but I wasn't sure if anyone else noticed that or if it was just me. And then there was the almost-deaf thing, but I figured that was just because he was old. No big deal. Other than that, what could anyone tease Mr Charles about?

"Ha!" he hooted. "Of course I have. I get laughed at all the time, son. Listen, I come from a family of Einsteins. My brother's a doctor. My sister's a big-time college professor at one of those smarty universities. Both my parents were lawyers. And me, I sell you sunflower seeds."

"What's wrong with that?" I asked. Shoot, having your own store seemed like a sweet deal. You never gotta pay for no groceries.

"Nothing is wrong with it. Not to me and you. But to them? Oh, they look at me like some kind of letdown. You know what they call this place? Charlie's *little* store," he said, his voice now more serious. "Little. Don't ever let someone call your life, your dreams, little. Hear me?" I nodded. He continued, all fired up, "Because while they're out there sniffing their own butts, I get to hang out with a big man, like you. A future World's Greatest. And that's cool." Mr Charles smiled big. Warm. "So we got a deal? No more skipping school?"

"No more skipping school," I agreed all quick.

He lifted his hand from the bag, but before I could take it, he slapped his hand back down on it.

"You're not just saying that to get the seeds, are you?" he said, now glaring.

"Nah, man. For real. No more skipping school!"

He let go of the sunflower seeds, and I snatched the bag before he changed his mind again.

But I didn't breeze on out of the store like I normally do. I was still kinda paranoid about being busted by the cops, slammed up against the wall, searched, caught with fancy running shoes in my backpack, and thrown in jail where the cafeteria food is worse than my school's *and* the hospital's. So I just hung around the store eating my seeds while Mr Charles went through inventory. He had just gotten a drop-off of new stuff: sodas, chips, cleaning products, cereal.

"You can't just hang out here, Castle. I mean, you're my guy, but you see that sign?" Mr Charles pointed to the one on the window. NO LOITERING.

"Ain't nobody loitering. You don't see me just spitting seeds on your floor or nothing like that," I protested. I opened my hand so he could see that I had been spitting them into my palm.

"No, not littering. *Loitering,*" Mr Charles said, ripping open a box. "Means you can't just stand around."

"Oh, well, you want me to help you with

some of these boxes?" I asked, hoping he'd say yes, because the only other place I could go was the bus stop, and that was too out in the open. Either that or the track, but I was going to end up there later anyway, and after yesterday, I wasn't down for another double practice. Plus, if the cops were out looking for a kid who stole running shoes, they might show up where the kid might be using them. So it was best to not be out there in the middle of the day, alone.

Mr Charles studied me for a moment, then thrust a box of cat food in my arms. "Here, help me unpack this."

The process was simple. There should be five of everything, everywhere, which was really just a weird way for Mr Charles to keep the store looking neat and organized, and also an easy way for him to know if people were stealing from him. So for instance, in the fridge, there should be five of every soda. Five of every juice. On the cereal shelf there needed to be five of every kind of cereal, even the nasty ones that taste like dirt until you put sugar on it. Same went for chips and cookies. So my job was to look around the store and let Mr Charles know what was missing.

"We need two orange juices," I said, thumbing through the juices like I was looking for a shirt in the coldest closet ever. Mr Charles, as usual, didn't hear me. I looked over; he was reading another piece of paper. This time it was one that he pulled from a box. I think it was like a receipt or something to tell him what he was supposed to have in each carton. He never even looked up, didn't hear me at all. Dang. I wonder what it must be like to be hard of hearing. I bet gunshots sound like knocks on the door, which is a scary thought. Sheesh. Anyway, I repeated myself, louder. "Mr Charles!" This time he looked up. "We need two orange juices." Mr Charles nodded, pulled two from a box, and handed them to me.

Of course, while we were doing all this, I kept an eye on my backpack. I had set it down in a corner at the back of the store. Every time we'd restock some cookies or some dishwashing liquid, I would doublecheck to make sure it was still there, that my sweet

108

silver babies were still safe.

After the counting and restocking was done, Mr Charles asked me to move all the leftovers into the stockroom.

"No problem," I said, struggling to get a grip on the sides of one of the bigger cardboard boxes. "Is there any order you want me to put them in?"

"Nope," Mr Charles said, now wiping down the counter. "Just stack it all up toward the back so I can get in there and move around. That's all."

One by one, I picked up boxes of ramen noodles, six-packs of beer, and cases of Worcestershire sauce (*war-sess-ter-shyer* . . . *worst-tester-shier* . . . gotta be a world record for hardest word) and moved them into the stockroom. Mr Charles seemed to have relaxed and was now standing behind the counter, staring at his old TV again. That made me feel kind of good, like I was doing something to help the old man out. I mean, he had always been so cool to me, such a good guy, so it felt nice to be able to do something for him.

Plus, he was getting up there in age.

He even had that weird, flappy, turkey-neck thing. So lifting these boxes was probably getting pretty hard for him.

The sixth (or was it the seventh?) box was the heaviest. It was filled with gallons of water, which was crazy because it just doesn't seem like water should be that heavy. I mean, it's clear. Like air. And air don't weigh nothing. I couldn't even really lift the box. I just held my arms straight and did the caveman walk to the stockroom, bumping into everything, including the stockroom door, hoping I'd make it there before my shoulders popped out the sockets.

The door closed behind me. I dropped the box and used my feet to slide it across the room over to the other boxes. Then I stopped and, for the first time, had a look around.

I can't tell you that I remember anything about what the stockroom looked like when me and my mum hid in it. But I know we were in the corner, a corner where there was now a coatrack. I remember that me and Ma huddled right there, up against the wall, her holding me by the face, her hands covering my ears. Now when I think about it, I think she did that so that I wouldn't hear her crying or breathing hard, even though I could feel her chest rising and falling at the exact same pace of my own thumping heart. But I don't remember there being any boxes. I don't remember the desk and file drawers, the clock on the wall or the five-dollar bill hanging in a frame. It all might've been there, but I just don't remember seeing it. And looking at it then, gazing around the room, I didn't really feel nothing. Like, no emotions. Until . . . I tried . . . to open . . . the door.

It wouldn't budge.

I tried again.

The knob turned, but the door wouldn't come loose. I knocked lightly, trying not to panic. But of course, Mr Charles couldn't hear me. He was probably deep into his cowboy flick. And he was on the other side of the store. And on top of all that, he was practically deaf. So I banged. Still nothing. Then I started trippin'. Like how when you at the swimming pool on the hottest day of summer, and you jump in and it's cool, and then you take one step too far and suddenly you're in the deep end, and things ain't so cool no more. Because you can't swim. That's how I felt. Like I was drowning. Like I was filling up with water. Like this place, this weird little room that had saved my life, now felt like it was gonna take it.

I looked at that corner again, my mind boomeranging back to me and my mum crouching and crying, wondering if my dad would corner us. My heart began to hammer just like it did back then. The clock on the wall suddenly seemed to tick louder. I turned back around and beat on the door again. Tried to beat a hole through it. Balled my hand into a fist and pounded and pounded and pounded, yelling Mr Charles's name until at last, after what seemed like forever, I could hear him on the other side of the door.

"Castle! I'm here," his voice came through, muffled. Mr Charles pulled it a few times, each time letting out a weird grunt, until finally the door swung open. He stumbled back into the chip display, before finally catching his balance. I shot out of the room.

"Stupid thing gets stuck," he tried

explaining, but I couldn't wait around to hear about it. One more minute and I would melt in the aisle between the crisps and the sodas, so I grabbed my backpack and ran straight for the door.

6

WORLD RECORD FOR THE LONGEST RUN AFTER THE MOST RUNAWAYS IN A SINGLE DAY

I RAN NONSTOP to my next stop, which was the track. But not only because I was buggin' about being trapped in a stockroom – *that* stockroom – and trust me, I was buggin', but also because that creepy clock reminded me that I was also late for practise. I ran through the streets until I finally made it to the park, where everyone was already warming up.

"So nice of you to finally join us, Mr Cranshaw," Coach said as I threw my bag down. I wanted to tell him that I'd basically been trapped in a teleportation thingy that zapped me back to the scariest moment of my life, but I didn't because I knew no one would believe me. So I just sat down on the bench, kicked my half shoes off – thankfully, everybody else was focused on stretching, and not on my feet – and rolled my trouser legs up.

"Sorry, sorry," I said, unzipping my bag, but Coach had already turned his attention back to the other runners. I looked to my left and right, then over my shoulder, then quickly scanned the other side of the track to make sure there were no extra guests dressed in undersized navy-blue uniforms with badges and handcuffs checking out practise. Once I knew the place was clear of cops, I pulled the silver shoes out and slipped them on my feet, lacing them up tight. Then I threw the beat-up trainers in the bag and hit the track.

"So today is Thursday," Coach said as I sat down to join in on the much . . . *much*-needed stretching. After spending the day with fire in my legs, stretching made so much more sense now. It took maybe two seconds for Patty to notice my shoes. She smiled and slapped Sunny on the arm to get his attention. Then he saw them and gave me a thumbs-up. So corny. I looked over at Lu. He was staring at them and fixed his mouth in the way people do when they're thinking, *Not bad*. And that was good enough for me.

Coach continued, "And Mikey, tell 'em . . . uh . . ." Now Coach caught a glimpse of the diamonds on my feet and got stuck. He looked both surprised and confused. It was the same expression he had when I told him to call me Ghost. "Um . . ." He caught himself and continued, "Mikey, tell the newbies what we do on Thursdays."

Mikey said in his usual grunty way, "Long run."

"That's right. Long run," Coach said. "This is about conditioning. Not speed. And everybody has to do it."

Let me tell you, when he said, "Long run," there were a few things I *hadn't* thought about. The first was that I hadn't had lunch because of the whole running-out-of-school thing, and I was starving and wouldn't be able to eat until after practise. And the second was just how much I needed food to give me energy, because what Coach meant by long run was run a million miles. Especially since I'd just run about a million miles. From the school to the store, and the store to the track. Then a crazy thought hit me – was he punishing me for stealing even though he didn't even know? Or did he? Nah, he didn't. He couldn't . . . he didn't. This was just a coincidence. A bad, bad coincidence.

Coach didn't tell us how far we would be running or anything. All he said was follow Whit.

"Where you going?" I asked as Coach started walking toward his car. But he didn't say nothing back. That's when Aaron told me what was going on.

"He's getting in the Chase Mobile, or as he calls it, the Motivation Mobile," Aaron said, patting me on the shoulder. "You'll see." He ran in place for a few seconds. I copied him and did a few high kicks. I felt like a gump doing it, but all that went out the window when Aaron said, "Nice shoes, man." I was gonna tell him that I called them the silver bullets but decided that probably would've been too much. Plus, there was no more time for talk. Coach was honking his horn, which I guessed was the signal for the run to begin.

Coach Whit took off, and we all ran behind her off the track and out onto the sidewalk as if we were some kind of running mob of obstacle-course contestants, dodging people and car doors, ducking under store awnings and jumping over random bicycles. The pace wasn't anything too crazy. A little more than a jog, but definitely nowhere close to a sprint. And, honestly, I was surprised at how I kept up for at least ten minutes before starting to drop back. Had to be the shoes. Sunny was up front with some of the other distance runners, like Lynn, Brit-Brat, whose real name was Brittany, and J.J. Patty was in the middle, keeping pace with Deja and Krystal Speed. She seemed to be doing okay too. In the back were the sprinters, which made sense. The new shoes were definitely helping me out, but there was only so much they could do. At about twenty-five minutes, which was longer than I had ever run, I eventually fell behind the other sprinters, putting me in last place. And that's when I learned what the Motivation Mobile was.

First it was just a honk. One short toot. I turned around and there Coach was in his cab, his hazard lights on. I couldn't believe what I was seeing. He was trailing us!

Then came the long honk. Then the megaphone. Coach rolled his window down and started screaming at us – well, really just me – through it.

"Pick it up, Ghost! Pick it up!" he screeched, his voice loud and crackly. I won't lie: knowing that he was on my heels like that, watching every step I took, definitely put the pressure on. Made me feel like I was being chased, which is always the easiest way to keep running. I knew that. A couple hours ago I had been running from invisible cops. And there was that time I got chased by a dog, hanging out at the basketball court hoping somebody would pick me to run. This older guy that everybody calls Sicko was there playing. He's one of those guys with a crazy eye, who never goes nowhere without his dog. He had the fathead mutt tied to the leg of one of the benches, and when I went to go pet it (stupid, I know), it got to barking all crazy, jumping at me, snapping his mouth. I backed away, but it kept lunging until finally the leash popped. It just popped! That dog chased me around the court and off the court, and I didn't stop running until I got home. That might have been the fastest I had ever run. Well, the second fastest.

Anyway. I won't lie. I never caught up to everybody else, even with Coach pretty much yelling at me through that stupid megaphone the whole time. He was leaning on the horn like a crazy person, everybody on the street looking at me, some totally confused and some actually cheering me on. I didn't even come close to finishing with everybody else, but I didn't quit. I never stopped running.

As everybody except for Sunny lay down on the track, trying to catch their breath, Coach had this cocky grin on his face as he came from his car, like he knew he'd worked us to death. "Coach Whit, who shined today?" he asked, jingling his keys.

Coach Whit stood with her hands on her head, her face and the parts between her braids glistening with sweat. "I gotta give it to Sunny, Coach. The kid stuck with me the whole time." Sunny lit up. He wasn't even tired. Like running eight hundred miles or however many we ran was no big deal to him. I, and I'm sure almost everybody else, felt like, I don't know, like we had become slime.

"Good job, Sunny," Coach said, giving him a high five. "I told you vets to look out for him, didn't I?" Mikey and Aaron and Brit-Brat and J.J. and pretty much all the vets groaned, but I could tell they were impressed by lanky-legged Sunny. Patty jumped up and gave him five as well.

"Yo, you like an alien," she said.

"Yeah man, you got legs," Lu followed. Then he turned around to me. "You too, Ghost. Them new shoes ain't give you no new speed, but you ain't quit, so . . . yeah."

"Thanks," I said. "You too." I don't know why I said "You too." It's just like a reflex. It didn't even really make sense in this case, but that's what came out.

"Okay, okay," Coach said. "Y'all can hug and all that tomorrow at the newbie dinner."

"What's that?" Patty asked.

"It's tradition. Every year I take the newbies out for Chinese food on the first Friday of the season. It's like a bonding thing," Coach explained, and then looking from me, to Lu, to

Patty, to Sunny, one by one, he added, "What, y'all don't like Chinese food?"

Of course we quickly answered, "Nah, Chinese is good."

"Definitely."

"Sounds good to me."

"I'm cool with it."

Coach, with the key ring now on his middle finger, spun the keys like cowboys do with their guns on the old movies Mr Charles was always watching.

"Okay, then," Coach said. "Now give me two cooldown laps and get off my track."

At home, me and Ma had my favourite for dinner. Salisbury steak. Every time she brought it home, all I could think about was how lucky the people in the hospital were that they could get that for dinner. Salisbury steak is amazing. I don't know what exactly Salisbury is, but whatever it is, it's delicious.

"So you liking running?" Ma asked, heating the food up.

"Yeah, it's cool. It's crazy hard, but it's cool."

"And what about the coach?" she asked. "How's he?"

"I like him," I said, plain, unsure of what she was getting at. Like I said, mums never trust people around their kids. Never ever. And Coach had just left after asking my mum if I could go to the newbie dinner, and she said I could, but the smell of Salisbury might've changed her mind just that quick. I don't know why it would've, but who really understands mums?

"You know what?" she said, popping open the microwave when it dinged. She flashed a smile at me. "I like him too."

Phew.

The homework Ma was avoiding tonight was all about how to draw blood – they call it phlebotomy – and the movie of the night was *Love Jones*, which we've seen a *bazillion* times, but my ma loves it. It's about this photographer lady and this guy who writes poems and they like each other, then they hate each other, then they love each other, and then it's over. Or something like that. I never really pay much attention. I just flip through my world records book and spout out different facts.

"You know, there's this guy named Tommy . . . um . . . Tommy something." I couldn't pronounce his last name. "He holds the world record for pulling the most nails out of a piece of wood with his teeth."

My mother, sitting with the nursing textbook open on her lap, just shushed me and kept on watching.

"And there's this other guy," I continued, even though I knew she didn't want to hear it. Most of the time I just liked to mess with her. "His name is Wim Hof. What a name, right? Yikes. Wim Hof. Anyway, he got the record for the most amount of time spent in ice."

"In ice?" my mother asked. Must've caught her at a boring part in the movie.

"Yep. *In* it. One hour and fifty-three minutes."

"People crazy," she said, shaking her head. Then she held her hand out in front of me to let me know the boring part of the movie was now over – it was time for her to resume fanning the tears back every five minutes. Blah, blah, blah.

"Hey, you ever heard of Usain Bolt?" I

asked her. "He holds the record for being the fastest man."

"Cas, come on now," she begged. "They getting ready to fall in love again. You know this my favourite part."

I just shook my head and kept on flipping. The good thing was she didn't ask me about my new fancy shoes, but that's just because she didn't know about them. I changed them in Coach's cab on the way home from practise. Coach, on the other hand, definitely asked about them.

"Where'd you get 'em? That's all I wanna know," Coach said. This came after he told me that he was proud of me for not quitting today. I told him that I had no idea why he loved to torture children so much.

"Do you grill all the kids on the team like this? Or just me?" I replied, snappy.

"Just you." He slapped my arm.

I told him that my mother had gotten them for me as a way to encourage me to do the right thing and stay out of trouble. Just saying it turned my stomach, because here I was, a boy who was suspended for busting somebody in the face at school one day, and skipped half the day the next because I was laughed at. Then I swiped shoes! I clearly wasn't staying out of trouble. Matter fact, I was knee deep in it.

"Oh . . . okay," Coach said, but I could tell he didn't believe me. I wouldn't have. He could probably see it on my face, especially since just like him, I didn't have no hair on it to disguise it either. And honestly (yes, honestly), I couldn't even believe that I had just lied like that. I wasn't really the lying type. But I also wasn't the stealing type until a few hours earlier. Altercations, altercations, altercations!

7

WORLD RECORD FOR THE BEST FRIDAY EVER AFTER THE WORST WEDNESDAY AND THURSDAY

FRIDAY MEANS TWO things. The first is that it's the last day before I can take two days off school. I like to think of it as a non-altercation suspension. Plus the weekend was when me and Ma actually did stuff – and not just watch movies and avoid homework – because she didn't work on weekends and took early morning online nursing classes to get them out of the way. And when she was done, we would clean the house (I was in charge of the living room), Ma would give me her version of a haircut (she always got most of it even), then give herself one, and then we would go over my Aunt Sophie's house. Aunt Sophie is my mum's younger sister, and she's like the coolest lady ever. She has a tattoo on her arm that says SWEETIE PIE that I never asked about, but always stared at just because I can't wait to get one. But mine ain't gonna say nothing like that. Mine's is gonna say WORLD'S GREATEST or, of course, GHOST.

Anyway, on the weekends, Aunt Sophie and my mum sit around and play cards and crack jokes and eat tortilla chips with cheese dip and drink beer, and sometimes they let me and King, Aunt Sophie's son, sit with them and play. Yes, we can play. Me and King learned how to play spades and tonk when we were real young. It's a thing in our family. A serious thing. And yes, his real name is King. I think the sisters just wanted to give us royal names. So, yeah. All I had to do was get through Friday without any problems, and I was good to go for the weekend.

The other thing about Friday, which I didn't know until Thursday, is that Coach gives everybody the day off. No practise. And then, of course, since this was the first Friday of the season, Coach was taking the newbies out for dinner.

After two half days of school (which technically equals one full day), I'm happy to say that school went pretty smoothly on Friday.

Brandon Simmons was back, and even though I had on my regular dusty-butt shoes – the fancy ones were for running only – Brandon didn't have too much to say to me. I saw him just before first period, and he walked right past me and Dre. I saw some of the other kids snickering at him as he passed. But I told them all to chill. I don't know why because he totally deserved to be roasted, but I guess I felt kinda bad for the guy. I been there.

"I can't believe you're giving this clown a pass," Dre said. It was almost like he had a year's worth of laughs stored up, waiting to unload them on Brandon. Everybody did. But I just couldn't let it happen. Funny thing was when I saw Shamika in Mr Hollow's class, she apologized to me about everything that went on in class the day before. And that, my friends, is what they call karma. Plus, like I said, she was a cool girl anyway.

At lunch, she even sat with me, Red, and Dre, and told us every story about times she cut things, just because she was feeling a little guilty.

"There was one time I cut my hair. Man, that was crazy. Just straight-up started hacking it off like a maniac, just because it was hot and my hair was on my neck," she said first, just before taking a bite of her burger. Then, in the midst of chewing, she continued, "And another time, I cut a pair of jeans into shorts while I still had them on! That was *not* smart! Still got the scars on my legs!" And then she erupted into laughter just like she did in class. But this time she was the butt of her own joke. And even though me, Dre, and Red didn't really find it that funny, we couldn't help but laugh too because, well, that's what her laugh makes you do.

Before I knew it, school was over and I went on my usual walk home. I mean, Coach wasn't coming until later, so I figured there was no rush. So I went to Mr Charles's store.

"Let me guess, sunflower seeds?" Mr Charles said. He turned the little TV down as usual.

"Let me guess, a dollar?" I said, slapping my money on the counter. I grabbed the bag.

"You okay, son?" Mr Charles asked.

"Yeah, why?"

"Oh, you know . . . all that stuff that happened yesterday with you being teased, and then you came here and got . . ." He stopped short.

I was starting to feel a little annoyed that he even brought it up, because I was definitely trying to forget about it all. Especially that last part. The stockroom part. Talk about *weird.* Not that I hadn't thought about it. I mean, how could I not? But every time my father's face, or the sound of his angry voice, or the sound of the gun cocking popped into my mind, I would just shake it out of my head by thinking about *my* bullets. The *silver* bullets. But you just can't be mad at an old James Brown–faced man like Mr Charles. You just can't.

"Yeah, man," I assured him. "I'm cool. I'm actually in a good mood."

"Oh yeah?" he asked.

I used my teeth to rip open the corner of the bag. "Yep. Got a dinner thing I'm going to tonight. For my running team," I said, all proud.

"Running team?" Mr Charles asked, now turning the TV down even more. "You're on a running team, Castle?"

"Yes, sir," I started to say, but it's hard to try to talk and get a seed out the shell at the same time. So I waited until I got it done, then continued, "Remember, I told you yesterday?"

"You did?" Mr Charles looked puzzled. "The old brain's getting wonky these days. Sorry, son."

"It's cool." I tapped the bag in my palm to get a few more seeds out. "So yeah, I'm on a team called the Defenders. One of the best teams in the city."

"I didn't know you were an athlete." Mr Charles seemed impressed.

"Well, I am. A pretty good one too," I bragged, tossing the seeds in my mouth, then casually slapping my hand against my thigh to brush the salt off. A shock of soreness shot down to my knee, a painful reminder that I was definitely an athlete. *Argh!*

Mr Charles twisted the top off a cranberry juice and took a sip. "I believe you. I told you, kid. You're one of the world's greatest."

"Got that right," I said, now spitting shells in my hand. "One of the world's greatest."

After I left the store, I headed to stop two – the bus stop. I took a seat next to an older woman.

She was doing a crossword puzzle and humming a song I didn't recognize. She might've been making it up. It didn't sound bad, though. Across the street at the gym were all the people working out – the Walking Dead. Ha! That's what they look like! Anyway, I hung out there for a little while before moving on. When I got to Martin Luther King Park, I looked down at the running track and there wasn't nobody there except for a man jogging with his dog. But nobody else. No *real* runners. After that, there was really no place else to go but home, and I wasn't ready to go there yet. So I went to the basketball court.

At the court, as usual, all the older guys were there running fives for cash. I knew some of them just because they were always there playing. Like Pop, who was probably in his twenties or something like that. I don't even think he was anybody's dad, but everybody called him Pop anyway. He was a short dude, with crazy handles, and a mean jumper. He was one of those guys who could do all the tricks and stuff. Shake you right out your socks like it was nothing. And Sicko was there too, but luckily for me, he didn't have his crazy dog with him. Sicko wasn't really that good at basketball, but he was super rough. He probably should've been a football player. Or a wrestler. Big James was there too. He was like the best player ever to me. He looked like he really played pro ball. Six feet something, all muscle. People always said Big James played college ball but never went pro. I never knew what he did for a living. All I knew was that he was always at the court, dominating the game, taking everybody's money. So I guess basketball was what he did for a living after all.

Besides the hoopers, there were a whole bunch of other people at the court, just hanging out. Girls. Some were the girlfriends of the guys playing, and others wanted to be the girlfriends of the guys playing. And junkies. They'd just be zombied out, roaming around the outside of the court. They knew better than to mess up the game. They'd just walk along the out-of-bounds line like it was a tightrope, waiting for Goose. Goose was the dope man, who also happened to be a pretty good ballplayer. Super flashy, but an all-around nice guy. Well, except for selling drugs. The court was where he served, in more ways than one.

I chilled there for a while, watching Sicko push everybody around until what always happens happened. A fight. As usual. Stupid Sicko pushed the wrong guy. A guy I didn't know. And that guy pushed Sicko back. And then Pop got into it. And then Big James. Then Big James's girl. And then some other girl. And then a junkie started howling like a wolf. And then I was out.

By the time I made it home, I only had a little bit of time to kill before Coach picked me up. Just enough time to wash up, or as my mum says, splash some water on my hot spots, throw on some clean clothes, and give myself two spritzes of perfume. It was Ma's, and it smelled like flowers, but hey, so what.

When Coach showed up, he hit the horn a few times. And when I didn't come right out, he hit it a few more times.

"I'm coming, I'm coming," I said, locking the door. Coach had his window down and was talking to Mr Jefferson, the neighbourhood sweeper. At least that's what we called him. He basically swept up the street every single day, but it didn't seem to ever really get clean. There was always glass, or paper, or, I don't know . . . a dirty couch.

"Wassup, y'all," I said to Patty, who sat up front, and Lu who was in the back with me. I wondered where Coach put all the junk that was usually in his cab. Probably in the boot, which was a place I never, ever, ever wanted to see.

"Wassup, man," Lu said.

"I been around here before," Patty said, skipping the hello. "I can't remember when. But I know I been around here."

"Me too," Lu said. "Not really these parts, but my pops plays ball sometimes at the court down the street."

"Oh yeah? I play at that court," I lied. Man. I was getting smooth with the lies. "Just came from over there."

Coach shook Mr Jefferson's hand, then turned around to me. "Took you long enough," he tossed over his shoulder. Then he sniffed, and sniffed, and sniffed. "That's you smelling like flowers?" Coach asked Patty.

"Nope, that's pretty boy back there," she said.

"Who, Lu?" Coach adjusted his mirror.

"No, the other one," Patty said, talking about me. I couldn't even believe she called me pretty boy. I squeezed my cheeks to crush my smile. And before Coach or Lu could say something slick, Patty added, "I like it. Smells good."

One more stop before the Chinese food. We left Glass Manor and went to the other side of town. Like, the other, other side. Where the houses have yards in the front *and* the back. Where there are two or three floors and each kid has their own room. Even if there are like five kids, each one gets their own four walls. And everybody has a car. Or two. And there are driveways to park those cars in. And there are also basketball courts in those driveways, the kind you can move around and adjust to make it low enough to dunk on. No wig shops, no fish markets, no Mr Charles, which had to suck. And as we pulled up in front of Sunny's house, a big brick castle with an old rusty car in the driveway, I wondered why Sunny didn't act like the other people I'd met who lived in this neighborhood. He was . . . cool. A little weird, but cool.

Coach hit the horn. Sunny came right out, tall and awkward. He waved to us, that funny wave he always did.

"Yo, Patty, you should get back here so Sunny can actually get his legs in the car," Lu suggested. I agreed. It didn't make sense for Sunny to be cramped up in the back with us. Plus, Sunny had already opened the back door on my side, and I just wasn't into sitting in the middle.

"Yeah, Patty," I said. "That makes the most sense."

"I don't care what y'all do, just do it quick so we can go," Coach barked.

Patty turned around and looked us up and down. "Ain't nobody sitting back there with y'all goons. I might get goon juice on me, and don't nobody want goon juice on them. What if I can't get it off me? Then what?"

"Patty!" Lu yelped. Patty turned back around, ignoring him.

"Patty, come on," I begged.

"Seriously?" Lu whined.

At this point, Sunny had already started stepping in, forcing me to scoot over to the middle. The middle sucks. It's where babies sit, and I'm no baby. Sunny crunched and scrunched his body until he got it all in there. It reminded me of this guy Yogi Laser I read about who holds the record for having the fastest time to cram into a box. Crazy. Sunny's knees were smashed against Patty's seat, and he had no place to put his arm, so he had to put it around me. It was all just ridiculous. Once Sunny closed the door, which took three tries, Patty and Coach turned around to look at us.

"Awww, look at y'all. Bonding like brothers," Coach jabbed.

"Or like clowns!" Patty followed with a hook.

"Just drive, please," I groaned, seeing Sunny smiling away, like nothing was wrong, out of the corner of my eye.

8

WORLD RECORD FOR HAVING THE BEST SECRET

THANKFULLY, IT DIDN'T take too long to get to the Chinese restaurant. After we finished staring at the big orange-and-white fish swimming around in a giant tank in the waiting area, we found out Coach had our seats prearranged. He and Sunny sat on one side of the booth, and me, Lu and Patty sat on the other side. The weird red vinyl seats squeaked as we all shuffled in.

"Okay, so you guys, pick anything you want on the menu," Coach unbuttoned the top button of his shirt. "Anything at all. We're here to celebrate the newbies."

I didn't know how anybody else felt about picking anything on the menu, but I almost flipped out, I was so excited. I mean, I had been eating hospital food almost every day during the week for, I don't even know how long. I guess, since my dad had been gone. So this was going to be heaven.

We all checked out our menus. Way more than what I usually see when me, Mum, King, and Aunt Sophie order in on the weekends. Me and Mum always get shrimp fried rice, Aunt Sophie gets crab sticks, which I always thought was a weird choice, and King nine times out of ten orders a cheeseburger with two egg rolls. And when the food comes, me and King always throw the fortune cookies at each other and try to whack them to pieces with the chopsticks.

"Is everyone ready to order?" A waitress had come over, pad in hand, to scribble whatever we said.

"I am," Coach said.

"Me too," Patty said, closing her menu.

I was ready too. Lu looked like he was still thinking about it, but we figured he'd be ready by the time the waitress got to him.

"I'll have the shrimp lo mein," Coach said. "With a Sprite."

"Sesame chicken," from Patty. "And to

drink, do you have Cherry Coke?"

"Cherry Coke?" Lu bawked. "Who drinks Cherry Coke?"

"I do," Patty said, holding her hand in front of his face to shut him up.

"Ummm." The waitress thought about it. "I can put some cherry juice in a regular Coke. How about that?"

"Perfect," Patty said, smiling.

Lu moved her hand away.

"And for you?" The waitress was talking to him now.

"Oh, I'm not ready," he said, picking up his menu again. "Go 'head, Ghost."

"I'm gonna have the Peking duck, please. And a lemonade."

"Peekin' duck?" Lu, again.

"Not peeking," Sunny said. "Pe-king. I'll have that too, please."

"And to drink?"

"Sparkling water, please."

"Y'all are the fanciest newbies I ever met," Coach said. He moved his silverware and chopsticks off his napkin, then put the napkin in his lap.

"Are you ready now?" the waitress asked Lu. Again.

"Yeah, you ready?" Patty repeated, way harder than the super soft-spoken waitress.

"There's just so many options, but I think I'm just going to have shrimp fried rice," Lu said.

"Shrimp fried rice?" from Coach.

"After all that, you order shrimp fried rice?" from Patty.

"Good choice," from Sunny, nice-ing it up as usual.

The waitress disappeared with our menus. That's when Coach started his boring speech about how proud he was to have us on the team, and how great the season was going to be. He said we all showed promise. Well, that was something I had never heard before. That I was showing promise. Then he started dishing dirt about some of other teammates. Not really dirt. Just funny stuff they'd never tell us. Like how Krystal Speed used to be Krystal "No Speed." He said she used to run like her feet were made of cement. Now she's better. He also said Mikey has always been kinda tough. Comes from a military family. Coach said his father makes him salute and everything. Aaron is the oldest of a whole bunch of brothers and sisters. So he's always annoyed at everybody on the team but can't help but take care of everyone, which is why he's the captain. Right when he was telling us about how Curron Outlaw was the king of the false start last year, our waitress returned to the table with our food. Yes! It was go time. And I was so ready. I had even made up in my mind that no matter how good the food was, I would save some for Ma. I mean, it wasn't every day we ate duck. Matter fact, we never ate duck. So, yeah. I was definitely going to save her some.

We all put our napkins in our laps like Coach did. And as the lady set the plates in front of us, piled up with Chinese goodness, Coach quickly gathered all our forks and knives. He even snatched our chopsticks.

"Okay, newbies. Here's the deal," he said, clutching the utensils. "In order for you to get your silverware back so that you can enjoy this amazing food, you have to tell everybody one thing about yourself that most people don't know. Something good."

"Wait. What?" Patty said, looking longingly at her sesame chicken.

I stared at my duck, the smell of it doing all kinds of cartwheels and backflips in my nostrils. Oh, man.

"It's tradition," Coach explained. "So, who's first?"

"Me!" Lu offered, staring at his fried rice like it wasn't . . . fried rice. "I'm starving, so I'll go first."

Coach shifted one fork, one spoon, one knife, and one set of chopsticks in his right hand. The rest were in his left. He held Lu's utensils up and smiled. "Let's hear it."

Lu looked off, as if his secret was on the other side of the restaurant. Or in the big fish tank.

"Well," he started, giving us his attention again. "I'm albino."

"Duh!" Patty groaned, slapping her hand on her forehead. "He said a *secret,* fool!"

I wanted to chime in and say that if he had told me that a few days earlier, it actually would've been a secret to me. But then I would've had to admit that I thought he might've been an alien, and that wasn't exactly the secret I was wanting to share.

"Yeah, I already knew that," Sunny said softly.

"So did I," Coach said, putting the silverware in his right hand back in his left.

"Wait," Lu said, clearly fearing that his meal would be held up. That fried rice must've been calling his name. "Okay, okay. For real this time." He took a deep breath. "I always wanted a brother. But my mum can't have no more kids. And the reason why I wish I had one is because then I could've seen what I would've looked like if I wasn't . . . albino."

Me, Patty, Sunny, and even Coach went dead quiet. Nobody said nothing. Like, whoa! Plus, I could relate to wanting a brother too. It would be nice to have somebody to hang with during the week. I had King on the weekends, but on the weekdays it was just me and Ma, so mainly just me, because she's Ma, and Ma ain't bro. Plus, I probably would've had less altercations because my brother could've talked me out of some of them. He probably would've talked me out of cutting my shoes up and stealing the silver bullets from the sports store too. So I was totally with Lu on this one.

Coach handed Lu his utensils and even slid the soy sauce over.

"Don't wait for us, son," Coach told him. "Dig in. You earned it."

Lu went for it. As he shovelled rice into his trap, Sunny spoke up.

"So, I don't have a mum," Sunny said. "I mean, I do, but she's gone. She passed away giving birth to me."

Patty's eyes instantly began to shine. I could feel mine wetting up too, but I didn't want to cry. Not at our special newbie dinner. But I felt for Sunny. My mother isn't always the happiest lady on earth, but that's just because times have been tough. But I'd rather have tough times with her than no times at all. Sunny ain't never even met his mum. Never even had her cooking, and all mums can cook (when they're not too tired).

"That's so sad," Patty said, reaching across the table for Sunny's hand. "I'm so sorry."

"Nah, it's okay. It's the reason I run. Well,

I didn't really have a choice. My father made me. See, he did everything right. Got good grades, went to college, became a big-time businessman, and found the perfect wife. They had the big house, and the nice cars, but my mother wasn't into any of that stuff. At least this is what my father says. He says that even though he gave her everything, she wanted to accomplish her own goals. And the biggest one was, she wanted to win a marathon."

"That's it? She wanted to run a marathon?" Lu asked with a full mouth.

"No. She ran a lot of them. She wanted to *win* one," Sunny clarified. "And she was planning to rev up her training after the pregnancy. But she died. So my father made me run. He felt like I owed it to her. I hated it at first, but I didn't have a choice. But now because I've been running for so long, I don't even think about it anymore and kinda feel like I can somehow connect to her this way."

"So your daddy used to run you?" I asked.

"Pretty much."

"But was it to punish you?" I darted

my eyes from Sunny to Coach, who sat listening closely.

Sunny's face started to pale. "I guess."

"But ain't that child ab—"

"Ghost," Patty cut me off, still holding Sunny's hand.

"Sorry, I didn't mean it like that," I backed off. "I was just saying, you know there's someone else at this table who might be guilty of doing the same thing. Running kids for punishment." I gave Coach a dramatic glare and everybody laughed, lightening the mood.

"Hey." Patty focused back on Sunny. She let go of his hand and readjusted herself in the booth. "I totally understand. I mean, I get it. Not the punishment part, but the part about your mum. My secret is sorta like that too."

Sliding Sunny's utensils over to him, Coach nodded but didn't say nothing. He just listened and doled out the eating tools. He put another set in his right hand. Those were going to be Patty's.

"Really?" Sunny said encouragingly.

"Yeah. I'm adopted, as all y'all already know," Patty continued. "But I'm not like most adopted kids. Most don't know their folks. But I know my mum."

"You do?" Lu asked, with a mouth full of rice this time. He looked so surprised, like he should've known this about Patty since they had been friends for so many years.

"Yep. Me and my little sister, Maddy, go see her all the time," Patty said. "She's cool."

"So why she give you up then?" Lu said stupidly.

"Lu!" Coach snapped. Lu stopped chewing. Coach pointed at me and Lu – why was he pointing at me! – and said, "Thing One and Thing Two, what y'all do before I picked y'all up? Study the world's most inappropriate questions?"

"No, it's okay, Coach," Patty said. "It's actually a good question." She rested her hands on the table. "She actually gave us up because she doesn't have legs. They had to get cut off because she got the sugar." Patty paused to make sure we knew what she meant by the sugar. I guess our faces made it clear that we didn't, because she continued, "Diabetes."

"But who takes care of her?" I asked.

"She takes care of herself, mainly. But she

couldn't take care of us, y'know," Patty explained, now fingering the corners of her eyes.

"So you run . . . for her," Sunny said, now understanding how Patty could somehow relate to his story.

"Yeah." Patty swallowed. "I run for her."

Coach handed Patty her silverware. "That leaves you, Ghost," he said. And let me tell you, I still wasn't sure what my secret was going to be, but I definitely knew I had to think of it quick, because my duck was getting cold, and cold duck didn't sound too good. At first I was going to tell them about the shoes. That I stole them. But then I figured Coach would not be okay with that, and even though he said we were telling secrets that we all were going to keep, I had learned a long time ago that adults play by different rules. So that was out. But I only had one other real secret. And I didn't know if it was okay to tell, especially over Chinese food. But I couldn't make up a good lie, despite the good job I had been doing lying over the past few days. I just didn't want them to look at me different or give anybody anything to pick on me about. I mean, I technically was still getting to know them, but I didn't *know* them know them yet. I didn't *know* know anybody besides my family. I never even told Red and Dre stuff like this. Matter fact, I hadn't even mentioned to them that I was on a running team, just because I didn't wanna have to go through the whole, *You? You on a running team?*

But then I looked around the table. Everybody had told such personal stories about their families, so maybe my family story wouldn't be so bad after all. Plus, um, my duck . . . it was getting cold. So . . .

"My dad's in jail for trying to shoot me and my mother," I blurted. And before anyone could say anything, I held my hand out for my utensils.

Lu dropped his fork.

Patty dropped her knife.

Sunny stopped drinking.

Coach's mouth hung open as he pressed everything into my hand.

And I felt . . . good. Different. Like,

even though they were all stunned by what I said, I felt like they could see me. Like we were all running the same race at the same speed. But I was also feeling pretty hungry.

"Thanks," I said, taking my fork and stabbing the duck with it. I twisted meat off the bone and stuffed it in my mouth like nothing was wrong. Like I hadn't just dropped the atomic bomb of secrets. But I didn't really want to make a big deal of it. I just wanted to say it and eat.

"So what about you, Coach?" I asked through my chewing of the best food I had ever had. Ever. Duck. Who knew? Charlotte Lee could collect all the rubber ones she wanted. I was gonna set the record for eating the most real ones. I mean, it's basically like the world's greatest chicken or something.

Everybody else had started back digging in their plates, even though now things were definitely a little awkward. Just a little.

"Uh, what about me?" Coach replied at last.

"Well, what's your secret?" I asked, pointing the fork at him.

"No, no, no, this is about y'all. Not me."

"Come on, Coach," said Patty. "Don't be like that."

"Yeah, I thought coaches were supposed to set an example," said Lu.

"Watch it," Coach snipped, but jokingly.

"No offence, Coach," Sunny said. "But Lu's right."

"And Lu's never right!" Patty teased, reaching over and snatching Coach's chopsticks and fork.

Coach shook his head. "I can't believe this. You dirty little rats. But I like the fact that y'all are ganging up on me. That means my plan is working." He put his hands together like an evil villain. "You're bonding."

"Yeah, yeah, yeah," Patty scoffed. "Just get to the secret, or kiss your noodles good-bye."

Coach sniggered. "Okay, okay," he started. "Well, it's true, Lu. I did run in the Olympics. And I won a gold medal." Coach looked pointedly at each of us, one by one. "Okay? So, there," he said, snatching his fork and chopsticks back from Patty.

And the conversation for the rest of the night was pretty much all about the Olympics.

Coach didn't really say too much more about it. It was mainly just us talking about what it must've been like and all that. But I was glad that we were off my secret – it was like I had never even said anything about what happened with my dad, even though I did. I did. And it seemed like everybody at the table cared and didn't care at the same time. And that made me feel, for the first time, like I was one of them. They even asked me if I needed to borrow some practice gear, which I thought was nice, but I told them I was cool. That my mother was going to get me some soon, even though I hadn't even asked for none yet. Plus, I kinda wanted my first jersey and shorts to be the ones I ran my first race in. Which, I hadn't really even thought about until just then. But I appreciated them offering to look out for me. Not many people do that. I could add them to the list of my mother, Mr Charles, and, well, Coach. And it felt good to feel like one of the teammates. Like I was there – really, really there – as me, but without as much scream inside.

WORLD RECORD FOR CLEANING THE DIRTIEST CAR

ONE TIME IN gym class we had to do this thing for warm-up where Mr Perham made us form two lines, facing each other. Everybody had to reach out and hold the hands of the person standing in front of them. For me, that person was, of course, stupid Brandon Simmons. His hands felt slimy, as if he had just blown his nose into his palms, which he probably did just to be a jerk. After we all were holding hands, Mr Perham stood in the front of the line with his back to us.

"This is called a trust fall," he said. "I'm gonna let myself fall backward, and I'm trusting you all are going to catch me."

"Like stage diving?" Greg Dodson said.

Mr Perham turned around. "Pretty much."

For someone about to be all trusting, he

looked kind of worried. Shoot, I was worried for him. I mean, I wouldn't trust somebody like Brandon to catch nobody other than himself or Monique. But Perham turned back around, took a deep breath, and leaned back.

That's basically what the whole "you gotta tell a secret to eat" thing Coach pulled on us was all about. It was like a trust fall with words. A warm-up to being Defenders. By the end of the dinner, it seemed like we were all connected in some strange way that none of us had imagined, and it stayed that way as we came to practise on Monday.

"Awwww," Aaron teased, as me, Lu, Patty, and Sunny hung around talking to each other before the stretch. Coach and Whit were on the side of the track, having an extra-long conversation with Chris Myers's father. "Look at the newbies. All of a sudden y'all besties, huh? Let me guess, Patty told y'all a secret about how she got a crush on Curron." Curron grinned as the other players laughed.

"Ain't nobody got a crush on Curron!" Patty replied.

"Dang, Curron. You heard that?" Freddy

chimed in, pulling the drawstring on his shorts.

"Yeah, I heard her. What's wrong with me, Patty?"

Curron asked, fighting back his embarrassment.

"Sorry, Curron," Patty started. "But I don't like boys who jump the gun."

Everybody laughed and Krystal Speed gave Patty a five, then fired off a few finger guns at Curron. *"Pyewn! Pyewn!"*

"What you laughing at, Krystal No Speed? When's the last time you won a race?" Curron fired back.

"The last time I seen your mama," Krystal said. "Ain't never ran so fast, 'cause I ain't never seen something so *ugggly.*"

"Hey, hey, no need to bring anybody's mum into this," Sunny chimed in, struggling to get his voice to cut through the *oohs.*

"Oh yeah?" Curron was now feeling big. Being laughed at was getting the best of him. "How 'bout we talk about *yours,* newbie?"

"That's enough, Curron." Aaron, who started this whole mess, finally decided to step in and fix it. But it was too late.

"Nah, let's talk about Sunny's mother," Curron insisted, now sizing Sunny up. We all knew he was just joking and that whatever zing he was gonna attempt was just gonna be silly, but still, this was Sunny. His mother wasn't even alive, and I knew that. And to me, that fact made those jokes off-limits. I also knew Sunny wasn't the kinda guy to stand up for himself. So I did.

"Let's not." I stepped in front of Sunny and looked cold into Curron's eyes.

Curron faced me, trying to hold his square, but I could tell instantly that he didn't want what I had for him. "Y'all see this kid?" he said, turning around to the other vets. Patty and Aaron came up alongside me, joining me in protecting our friend.

"Yeah, we see him, and since you a cupcake, we suggest you leave him alone," Aaron said, shutting Curron down.

Then a hand clap. Slow. One. Then another. Then another. Coach was standing with Whit, clapping. "That was fantastic," he said. "Wasn't it, Whit?"

"I thought so," Whit replied, folding her arms across her chest.

"So many tough guys and girls on this team –" Coach stopped himself. "Wait, did I just call you a . . . *team?*" He started toward us. "That's what this is, right? *Right?*"

"Yes, Coach," Aaron said, instantly slipping back into his role as Coach's pet.

"Oh, so only Aaron knows we're a team?"

"We're a team, Coach."

"Yeah, Coach. We're a team."

"We're a team."

"So then act like it. You understand me? Each and every one of you." He waved a finger past each of our faces. "Act like it! Matter fact, learn from the newbies. Defend each other. They're not your opponents. They're your new family. And as you can see, they mean business." I looked at Patty, Lu, and Sunny and tried hard to totally grin. Then I looked at Curron and nodded as Coach commanded, "Now let's stretch it out. Toe touches. Everybody down."

After stretching and warm-up, the sprinters spent the rest of the practice doing fartleks, which sounds like fart licks. Funniest name ever. Fart . . . lick. HA! But it has nothing to do with licking farts. It just means you run three minutes at 80 per cent speed, and one minute full-out. Sounds easy, right? Try doing ten of them. It's harder than it sounds. Way harder. Trust me.

On the first few I was able to keep pace with Lu, Mikey, and Aaron, and on the fourth, I decided to prove a point and turned the jets on. We hit the final stretch, the last hundred metres, which was when we were supposed to run full-out, and I must've channelled my inner Usain and bolted to the end.

"Good job, Ghost!" Coach said, whistle still in his mouth, clasping his hands behind his back. I bent over as the other boys crossed the line. They all swung their hands toward me, dapping me as Coached continued, "You proved that you can get it if you want it. Now get back on the line." But I couldn't move. Because even though Coach had blown the whistle, I had blown my legs.

"I ca ... I can't," I panted just loud enough for Aaron to hear me. I dropped to one knee.

He grabbed my arm. "Yes, you can. Let's do it. You got some more in you." And even though he was the captain, and kind of a suck-up, and he'd been smoked by me – a stupid decision that didn't feel nearly as good as I thought it would – I knew he meant that. That I still had more.

Needless to say, the rest of practise was rough, and ended in me crawling from Coach's cab, barefoot, to the house, through the house, into the bathroom, and into the bathtub, where I basically let the hot water cook my muscles.

And that's how it was every Monday after. Every other day during the week was similar, but with a different routine. Coach had it set up so that we always knew what we were doing at practise every day. That way if he was late, or if Coach Whit wasn't around, we could – Aaron could – run the workout for the team.

So it went like this:

Mondays: Fart licks. Which for me meant an afternoon of running my legs to death, and an evening of boiling them back to life.

Tuesdays: Technique. How to come off the block. Elbows in. Open up your stride. Head up. Back straight. Glide, don't wobble; be a horse, not a penguin. Run *through* the finish line, not *to* the finish line. Blah, blah, quack, quack, wah,

wah, on the line, whistle, whistle, over and over and over again.

Wednesdays: Ladders. Four, three, two, one, one, two, three, four. Also known as, Don't Eat a Big Lunch day. Going from four to one was rough but most of us could crush it. Even me. It was heading back up the ladder that was the killer. *Go down, throw down. Go up, throw up.* The absolute worst.

Thursdays: Long run. Every week, a different route. Once I was finally able to keep up, it was kinda cool being part of the train of runners zooming down the pavement, dodging people, and bus stop benches, and fire hydrants, and trash bags, with the Motivation Mobile trailing behind. My only fear was that one day Coach Whit would lead us on the wrong route – the route that went past the sporting goods store, where I was probably a wanted fugitive. Sure, I could just turn my head or shield it with my shirt – pretend to wipe sweat – and nobody would know it was me. But the shoes? There was no disguising them. That girl, Tia, would know the sparkle of the silver bullets, easy. Luckily, we never went that way.

Fridays: Everybody's favourite day. Off. Thank God.

I had pretty much gotten used to everything and everybody. Mean Mikey, mumbling stuff. Aaron, the captain of the team, acting like the captain of the team, which at first I wasn't so sure I was going to be okay with. I mean, the guy had a big mouth. Like, *big* big. But he knew how to keep everybody together and motivated, which could get hard when you're on the side puking your guts out. And then there was the four of us. The newbies. Our special gang. I had gotten used to Patty and Lu snapping on each other and arguing. All. The. Time. I had gotten used to Sunny quoting some spacey book that nobody had ever read. Or saying something really cool, but it's so out there that you don't really even know why it's cool, but it's cool. Matter of fact, I think that's the record he holds. The record for saying the coolest *what in the world is he talking about* sayings. Definitely. I had even gotten used to Coach on my back every day about my homework, which I usually got done during the ride home, and whatever I didn't, I finished while Ma was zoning into the cheesy movie of the night. Even Coach's stupid whistle and the constant shouting of "on the line" became just as normal as sunflower seeds from Mr Charles's store. I had got used to it all, and I was pretty sure that they had all got used to me. So everything was cool. Maybe the coolest it had ever been.

But uniform day changed everything. Uniform day was the day when Coach was going to give us our jerseys and shorts. He had been talking about this day for two weeks, going on and on about how uniform day was important because it meant you were officially on the team. It was the last piece to the puzzle. And I wanted that piece. I mean, I had traded running in my jeans for a pair of cutoff scrubs I got from my mum, but that was like running in a pair of drawers! And when I got to sweating . . . man, straightup gross. So a uniform sounded amazing. An actual uniform, just like basketball teams, except for a track team. Yes.

Coach showed up at practise carrying the box. He dropped it on the track in front of us as we bent and stretched, getting ready for the usual "Technique Tuesday" routine work. I was gonna practice coming off the blocks, because it was where I needed the most help. It felt weird to not just stand up straight and run when I heard the whistle. But to bend down and press my feet against that metal . . . thing, was way weird.

"Bring it in," Coach said. "As you all know, our very first meet of the season is this Saturday. You've worked hard these past few weeks, and I'm proud of you. So to get you excited about smoking everybody this weekend, I'm giving out this year's Defenders uniforms."

We clapped it up as Coach folded the cardboard flaps of the box back. "When I call your name, come get your uniform and go put it with your stuff. Then give me some warm-up laps," he said. Then, one by one he called each runner forward. I was standing next to Lu, and when Coach called his name, I gave him a *way to go* nudge. He grabbed his gear, then jogged back and gave me five. The jersey, which he held up, was electric blue, with gold letters across the front, DEFENDERS. Underneath the word was a picture of a fist clenching a wing. It would go perfect with the silver bullets. I liked it. No, I loved it.

"Sweet!" Lu sang out.

"Man," I said, not really believing how good it looked.

Coach called out name after name. Outlaw. Speed. Lancaster. Farrar. Bullock. Fulmer. McNair. And after every name I'd say to myself, waiting, *Cranshaw, Cranshaw. Cranshaw.* Tate. *Cranshaw.* Hayes. *Cranshaw.* But Coach went on and on until he got to the last uniform. My uniform. But he never called my name.

"And that's it," Coach said. *That's it?* I knew my eyes were buggin'. *That's it?* Everybody was checking their jerseys out, putting them in their gym bags, or jogging around the track. But I was still waiting.

"What about me?" I asked. I didn't understand what was going on. Where were my shorts? My jersey? Where was my uniform?

"Oh!" Coach said, as if suddenly remembering that he had left me out. But how could he have left me out? I had proven myself. I was pretty much the best sprinter on the team. At least one of them. Whatever. Didn't matter, I thought, because I had reminded him. "Oh right, I have something for you, Ghost," Coach said, digging back in the box. When he pulled his hand from the brown cardboard, he wasn't holding no electric blue dopeness. Instead he was holding a piece of paper folded into a small square.

"What's this?" I asked.

"Unfold it and see," Coach said, his face changing, falling into that familiar look of disappointment, the way Principal Marshall's face does whenever I've had an altercation.

I unfolded it as quickly as I could because *what the* . . . and what I found on that piece of paper was the most shocking thing ever. It was a picture of me, dashing from the sports store. A close-up of my face, and underneath it, in red – big bold red – was the word SHOPLIFTER.

I looked up at Coach. My tongue had suddenly turned into a stone in my mouth. I couldn't breathe, like I had just finished running ladders, like I was going to puke up every sunflower seed I had ever eaten, and if there was ever a sunflower growing in me, it was definitely dying right then.

"I went to go pick up the uniforms at the sporting goods store, and guess whose photo was taped to the window?"

I didn't say anyhing. I couldn't.

"Guess!" Coach insisted, forcing me to say it. But I just couldn't. He snatched the paper back, ripped it into confetti. "That's your uniform," Coach said, holding his hand open so I could see the white confetti. "And since you can't wear this" – he turned his hand over and let the paper fall to the ground like awkward snowflakes – "you can't run. So take your silver shoes and have a seat."

"Wait, Coach – "

"Sit!" he shouted, pointing at the wooden bench. Everybody looked at me as I started walking. But they weren't laughing, and instead just seemed shocked and concerned, which was probably the only reason I didn't take off running, away from the track, and off to the basketball court or Mr Charles's or anyplace else. Instead I did as Coach asked and sat down. "And for the rest of you, mind your business," Coach warned the team. "If I hear anything about this – anything at all – you can give your uniform right back. Am I clear?"

The team, shook about the prospect of

having to hand over their sweet new jerseys, grumbled and started their warm-up laps.

I stayed right there on that bench the whole practise. And Coach never once looked over at me, not even to check that I was still there. It was like he didn't even care. Matter of fact, I could've just got up and left, but that seemed like a bad idea, because I felt like if I left now, I could never come back, and my life on the team would be over. For good. So I just sat it out and hoped for the best. But I don't know what the best could've been. I was caught. Didn't really think it would happen. And even though I had already told Coach the shoes were a gift from my mum, I still had to tell my mum how I got them at some point, and I'd planned on telling her that Coach got them for me, and then hope and pray that she never thanked him. When I think about it now, that was the stupidest idea ever. Wow. Anyway, the point is I wasn't a thief. I mean, I guess I was. But I wasn't a criminal. I'd never swiped nothing before! I just needed some new shoes to run in.

After practise, everybody came over to me, doing the best they could to hold their words in but sending me all their *what did you do's* with their eyes. They each gave me five as they left, and it was like they were giving me my final five, the one that said, *We don't know what's about to happen to you, but hold your head up.* The one just before I'd have to walk the plank.

"Let's go," Coach threw at me, once everyone had left. His words knocked against my chest like knuckles. A two-piece. *Let's. Go.* I grabbed my bag and followed him to the car. As I opened the back door, he spat, "Up here," delivering two more to the ribs. He threw everything in the backseat as usual, then opened the passenger-side door. I closed the back door and got up front. As we rode through the city, neither of us said a thing. Coach didn't look over at me or nothing. He just bit down on his bottom lip, and occasionally he would shake his head like he was picturing the picture of me in that store over and over again. I thought about trying to explain myself, but what was I going to say? I didn't steal them? Because I did. So I just sat there, my legs becoming wooden with fear.

When we pulled up in front of my place, Coach cut the car off and opened his door.

"Where you going?" I asked, because he never got out the car except for the time he had to ask my mum if I could go on the newbie dinner, but that had been weeks ago. The routine was, he pulled up out front, dropped me off, waited for me to get inside, then pulled off. But he never, ever, got out the car.

"What you think I'm doing, Ghost? I'm going to tell your mother what you did."

OH. NO. I fumbled at the handle trying to get the door open and scrambled out of the car.

"Coach, no. Please," I begged. I ran around and got in front of him, holding my hands up as if I was trying to use some kind of magic force to push him back. Oh, man. I'm sounding like Sunny. But . . . hey. "Please, please, please," I pleaded, but Coach pushed past me. He was storming toward my house, and there was nothing I could do to stop him. I grabbed his shirt. "Coach!" He spun around. A tattoo I had never noticed before peeked from the now stretched-out neckline.

"Ghost," he said, his eyes closed. "I'm

only gonna tell you this one time. Let me go."
His voice was flat. Hard. Scary. I let his shirt go
and put my hands together.

"Please, Coach. You can't tell my mother."
It was like a rerun of the first Coach bailout when
he came and picked me up from school and I said
pretty much those exact words. And here I was
again asking him not to snitch on me. It's not
that I was scared of being punished or getting in
trouble with my mum. I was, but that's not why
I was begging. I just didn't want to add to the
problems. I mean, I'm her only child, the reason
she was working so hard, and I went out and
did something stupid. But the only reason I did
something stupid was because I knew I couldn't
ask her for the money. And the reason I couldn't
ask her wasn't because she wouldn't have gotten
the shoes for me. It's because she would have.
She would've done anything to get them. I knew
that. And I just didn't want her to have to give
up something – something else – for me to have
some stupid shoes. And now because I stole them,
she would be disappointed that I didn't come to
her and feel even more guilty. She'd think she
was a bad mum on so many levels. But I couldn't

just tell Coach all that. I didn't have the time. So I fell to my knees and pressed my hands together. "Coach, please. I know I messed up, but please. Please, Coach." The words began to break up in my throat. "Please."

Neighbours outside were looking at me act a fool. Coach noticed them too and knew that this just wasn't a good look, so he told me to get up and get back in the car.

"Just tell me why," he said, after slamming his door. He put his hands on the steering wheel and stared straight ahead. "Why, Ghost?"

"What was I supposed to do? My mother don't have no money for running shoes. I couldn't put that on her!" I replied.

"*Ask me!*" Coach said, now laser-beaming straight at me. I clenched my jaw as a marble of anger and frustration and fear rolled down my throat. "Why didn't you just ask me?"

"Because you're not my father," I snapped. "Why would I just expect you to help me? Why would you?" I felt like my entire body was now shaking. "I mean, you got me on the team, and thank you for that, and you bailed me out with my trouble at school and I thank you for that, too, but you . . . you . . . you just not . . . why you care so much anyway?"

"What are you talking about, Ghost? I care about all of you. Why you think I'm out there every day coaching y'all?"

"But I'm different. You know that. You heard my secret. You heard it. That ain't normal," I explained, my voice now straining, ripping into its own confetti. "And I get teased and laughed at all the time because I live here. And I look like this. You don't live here! You don't look like this!" Now stupid tears were welling up in my eyes. "You don't know what it's like, Coach. You don't know."

Now Coach swallowed something, like bitter air, twisting his face up. He turned his whole body toward me and pulled his shirt down so that the neck stretched even lower.

"You see this tattoo?" he asked. It was a dark band diving down into his curly chest hair. "It's my Olympic medal. I got a tattoo of it after the man who did this to me"—now Coach curled his top lip so I could see his chipped tooth—"stole the real one." Coach didn't give me a chance to say nothing, he just bulldozed on. "That man was my father. He was an addict. And every time he got high, he got violent. He punched me in the mouth when I was fifteen because I asked him to change the channel on the TV. The Olympics were on. And four years later, after I had worked my butt off to make something of myself, I got my shot to run in the same race I tried to watch when he hit me. And I won. It was the happiest moment of my life. And my mum's. And, I think, even my dad's. But three weeks later . . ." Coach paused, swallowed another dose of that bitter air, then continued. "Three weeks later, he . . . he sold my medal for a twenty-dollar high. And that was his last high. He overdosed, right over there on those steps." Coach pointed to a building a few buildings down from mine. Then he started tapping hard on the dashboard. "Because that's where we lived. That's where *I* grew up. So don't tell me what I know and don't know, Ghost."

I sat frozen in my seat.

"You from Glass Manor?" I asked softly.

Coach nodded. "That's how I know Mr Jefferson," he explained, which made a lot more sense to me now. "So I know what it's like to live here. I know what it's like to be angry, to feel, I don't know, rage on the inside."

Coach's face seemed to relax a little, like he was cooling down. "And the same thing running did for me, I felt like it could do for you." He looked out the front window and shook his head. "But maybe I was wrong."

"What did you think it would do for me?" I asked, realising that he never thought it could help me dunk by next year. Realising I didn't even really want to play basketball anymore.

He faced me again, looking straight in my eyes. "Show you that you can't run away from who you are, but what you can do is run toward who you want to be."

I let that sink in. Who was I? I was Castle Cranshaw, the kid from Glass Manor with the secret. The one with a daddy in jail and a mother who worked her butt off for me, and cut my hair, and bought knockoff shoes, and clothes that were big enough for me to grow into. I was the boy with the altercations and the big file. The one who yelled at teachers and punched stupid guys in the face for talking smack. The one who felt . . . different. And mad. And sad. The one with all the scream inside.

But who did I want to be? Well, that was harder to answer. I wasn't exactly sure yet. But definitely one of the world's greatest.

"Do you understand?" Coach asked, his head cocked to the side.

"Yeah," I replied sheepishly.

"Do you really?" He was glaring at me, hard.

"I do. Seriously." I wiped my face, sniffled, then added desperately, "But please don't tell my mum."

Coach sighed. "I won't." He paused, then followed with a threat. *This time.*

"Thank you," I murmured, so relieved I thought I was going to pass out. But I still had another question burning inside. "Well, do I still get to run?"

Coach glared even harder at me, and I was hoping that somewhere in my face he could see himself and give me another chance. I never wanted to be on a running team before I met him anyway. But now that I had been on one, even if it'd only been for a few weeks, I felt like I didn't want to do nothing else.

He unclenched his jaw. "Yeah, you can run." Then pointing down at my raggedy regular trainers, he added, "In those."

"But I can't—" I started, but Coach cut me off.

"You wanna run or not?"

"Got it."

"And Friday, you're cleaning my cab," he commanded.

"Coach!"

The rest of the week was pretty much filled with me being on my best behaviour at school – I was straightup acting like that annoying goody-good, Maureen Thorne – then working extra hard at practise, which was much more difficult than usual because running in my regular raggedy trainers made me feel like my feet had gained weight. Like I had obese toes or something. It had been a while since I had practised in my cutoff shoes, and I think the silver bullets had

off the team because his grades were slipping. Aaron was going to run the four hundred. He was the master of it. Like, seriously, could burn anybody. And between me and Lu, one of us was going to run the two hundred metre, and one of us was going to run the one hundred metre.

Now, here's the thing. The two hundred was a good race. A hard sprint. But it wasn't as, I don't know, glamorous. No, no, that's not the word. The two hundred just wasn't the . . . main event. The main event was the one-hundred-metre sprint. It was what Usain Bolt set the record in. It was *the* race. Before I got caught and Coach forced me to run in my old trainer, I had a pretty good chance at snatching that spot from Lu. Don't get me wrong, he was crazy fast and had been running that race pretty much ever since he started running. But over the month of practise, my time was maybe a half second faster than his. But not during the week of slumpy, cutoff shoe running, which was definitely the week that counted. But hey, it was only the first race of the season. So I figured I'd take the two hundred – honestly, I'd run any of the races Coach would let me – and work my butt off (and my legs and feet) to earn the chance to run that race.

Friday, Coach made me do exactly what he said I would have to. Clean out his cab. He came over to my house after school and drove around to the back of the building, where the bins were.

"Ghost, I'm not gonna lie to you," Coach said, popping the boot. "I don't know what might be in here."

I wasn't sure either. I mean, the backseat was pretty much clear, just because that was the part of the car that he rode customers around in every day until I got in the car after practise. Then he put all the stuff in the front seat in the back. So the trash went from back to front, then front to back. Fast-food bags, gym bags, paper, shoes, and who knows what else. And then there was the boot. When he popped it, and I looked in there and saw the end of the world, the backseat and front seat seemed spotless. The boot was ridiculous.

"Coach, this is crazy!" I said, staring into what looked like the black abyss.

"I know," he said, flashing an embarrassed

smirk. "I sure am glad you did a stupid thing and have to clean all this up."

And I did. I trashed all the fast-food bags, some with fries and half-eaten burgers still in them. I pulled out the duffels. I don't know why Coach needed so many gym bags. Who needs more than one? But there was nothing in them. They were all pretty much empty, because all the shoes, and stinky shorts, and towels took up about half the space of the entire boot! Dirty socks, and headbands, and old jerseys from past years with the Defenders. He also had starting blocks, which are big and metal and heavy, shoved in there. And whistles. Whistles everywhere. I opened up the gym bags and loaded them up with all that crud. When I got to the last one, a yellow-and-green duffel with the name Otis on it, I unzipped it.

"Who's Otis?" I asked Coach, who was sitting on the hood of the car, flipping through the lists of all our run times.

"Otis is me," he said, not even looking up.

"Oh," I said, flat. I mean, I knew Coach's last name was Brody, and I figured his first name wasn't just Coach. Nobody's name is Coach.

Well, that might not be true. My name is Castle, so someone might actually be named Coach, somewhere. But not chipped-tooth turtle face.

I started loading the bag up with a busted pair of cleats that probably would've been better off in the trash, when I spied a piece of paper, a crinkled-up rectangle, in the corner of the duffel. I pulled it out. It was a faded picture of a man, tall and slim like Sunny, facial hair only around his mouth but none on his cheeks. He had his hands resting on a little boy who stood in front of him. The kid was grinning. The man was looking away, almost like he was calling out for someone.

"Who's this?" I asked, bringing the picture around to the front of the car. Coach took it from me, looked at it like it was his long-lost gold medal. His mouth hung open for a few seconds before he finally answered.

"This is my father." He tapped the picture with his finger. "And that's me," he said about the happy little boy. "Where'd you find this?"

"In that bag."

Coach pulled the photo closer to his face, as if he was studying every detail. "Thank you," he said, and right then I got the feeling that being mad at his dad wasn't the only way he felt about him. He was. But I could tell Coach also missed his pops. He loved him. And I could totally relate to that, because as happy as I was that my crazy father wasn't around to hurt us no more, whenever he wasn't wasted, he was dope. That was my dad too. And I missed that version of him.

Coach gingerly slipped the photo in his back pocket, then pulled it right back out.

"Throw those bags in the trunk. I think you're done," Coach said, climbing into the cab. He took the photo and put it up in the dash part where the speed numbers are. I tossed all the gym bags full of dirty sports gear in the trunk and slammed it shut. Then I hopped in. "Where we going?"

"You'll see."

On the way to the land of *you'll see,* I teased Coach about the name Otis.

"Seriously, Otis is the name of old men who smell like cinnamon and barbecue sauce."

"Shut up, Ghost," Coach said, laughing.

"I mean, Otis is the name you give short, fat dogs. Not people."

"Oh, so I'm a dog now?"

"No, I didn't mean it like that."

"Well, how did you mean it?"

"I just meant Otis is a great-great-great-grandpa's name." I paused, struck by another thought. "Are you a mechanic? Because if you're a mechanic, then it's okay."

Coach pulled over on the side of the road. "You wanna get out?"

I zipped it. And my mouth stayed zipped until we pulled up right in front of – wait for it – Everything Sports. I looked out the window and into the store. Tia was there, leaning against the counter, checking her cell phone. She could be doing some high kicks or some jumping jacks, but no. She was texting. Not an athlete.

"Do I need to tell you what we're doing here?" Coach asked. And the truth is, he didn't. I knew why we had come. Why we had to come. *I* had to come. But it didn't feel good, that's for sure. Matter of fact, it felt pretty wack. I looked Coach in his eye and shook my head before exhaling a heavy, guilty breath.

"You ready?" he said.

"Yeah, I'm ready."

Coach walked in, and I trailed behind him with my head down, nervous and stupid feeling.

"Welcome to Everything Sports. Let me"—Tia stopped mid-greeting when she saw me. "Oh. It's you."

"Yes, yes, it's him," Coach said, his car keys clinking as he set them on the counter. I was still behind him, staring down at the grey carpet. "Head up, son. You know my rule," Coach coached. "Stand tall at all times."

I lifted my face and looked at Tia straight on. "I'm sorry," I started, and in that moment realised sometimes a real apology can go a long way. Just like Shamika's at school. Just like the one I never got from my father. But had he just told me he was sorry for what he'd done, maybe . . . I don't know. . . .

Coach was leaning his ear toward me like Mr Charles always did, as if he was hard of hearing. I followed up. "I'm really, really sorry for stealing the shoes. I just . . . I didn't mean anything. I made a stupid mistake."

"*Stupid* mistake. I mean, a *stupid, stupid*

mistake," Coach added, way too enthusiastic.

"That's what I said, Coach. Stupid."

Tia's mouth went from straight line to little bitty smile. Not big smile, but definitely not frown, and that was all that mattered.

"Okay," she said. "I forgive you."

Coach then handed over his credit card, and as Tia swiped it to pay for the shoes, Coach threw his arm around my neck, put me in a tight headlock, and whispered in my ear, "If you *ever* do this again, I promise I'll make room for you in the boot."

I looked him in his face, in his eyes. Not a flinch. Just that big chipped-tooth smile, and a scary wink.

Yikes.

10

RACE DAY

SATURDAY. RACE DAY. My first one ever. I got up early, met by the sweet smell of bacon and eggs, neither of which are actually sweet-smelling, but you know what I mean. My mother was on the phone with Aunt Sophie, telling her what time she had to be here so that we could all go over to Martin Luther King Park together. I didn't know what I was more excited about – the fact that I was going to run my first race on a track team, or the fact that my mother would be there to see it. I had been seeing Lu's mum cheering for every little stupid thing he did in practise, and after I got over how annoying it was, I realised that there was something about it I kinda liked. So, my mum being there was major. And Aunt Sophie, because she was the loud one. She was the one who had a bullhorn for a mouth.

"Don't be late, Sophie," my mum said into the phone, dishing out the eggs.

Of course, anytime a person tells another person not to be late, it pretty much guarantees that they will be. I don't know why, but it does. And Aunt Sophie was late. Not like crazy late, to the point that I couldn't make it to the track on time. It's just that we don't have a car and were going to have to catch the bus to the park. But the bus was supposed to come at 11:15, and Aunt Sophie and King didn't get to the house until 11:09.

I was in the bathroom, staring at myself in the mirror. Coach had given me my uniform the day before, after humiliating me at the sports store. Guess, well, I kinda humiliated myself. But whatever. When we got back to my house, he told me I had earned it and that he hoped he never had to bail me out like that again.

"I won't really put you in the boot," he said, smirking. "I'll just tell your mother and cut you from the team. That's *way* worse. Got me?" Coach dangled my jersey and shorts out in front of me. And I did get him. Big-time. I made up in my mind that I wouldn't nothing that stupid ever again. At least, I would try not to, especially judging from the way I felt holding that electric-blue uniform.

I usually get dressed in the living room, but I just wanted it to be a surprise for Ma when I came out. And I could've gotten dressed in the bathroom, but it's too small, and I couldn't risk doing anything stupid like dropping my jersey in the toilet or something. I know it sounds impossible; trust me, it's not. I mean, not like I ever dropped anything in the toilet or anything. But it could happen! So I did what I never do. I got dressed in my bedroom. I stood in the middle of the room with the door wide open and pulled my shorts on. Then my jersey. I looked around at the posters of LeBron on the wall, from when he played for Cleveland the first time. My bed. The same cover. Same pillow. Same everything as that night. I sat on it, my body sinking into the mattress, almost like it was wrapping itself around me, hugging me. Like it missed me. And if the door wasn't open and I couldn't see straight down the hall to the living room, I might've freaked out. But I didn't lose it. I just took a deep breath and let the flashes of that night come over me. My mother, flash, the covers being yanked off me, flash, the hallway, flash, the gun, flash. Then I looked down at the floor. Flash. My silver bullets, waiting for me. I unlaced them, slipped my feet in, then relaced them tight. And just like that, I felt different. I was a Defender.

My mother had even given me a fresh haircut the night before, just for this day, and I hit the bathroom to brush it and see if maybe a few waves were popping out. Or at least make sure it wasn't one of her jackedup cuts. Thankfully, she got it close to perfect. Almost no patches.

While primping in the mirror, I heard Aunt Sophie come in. She was hollering about how they were late because she had to make a sign to hold up when I was running.

"Castle!" my mother called from the living room. "They here! Let's go!"

I came out the bathroom and my mother almost hit the floor. She put her hand over her mouth, which I only ever saw her do when somebody on one of those movies said something corny about not wanting to live without the other person and then they kiss.

"Look at you," Mum said, hugging my neck, her eyes instantly wet. "You look like a champion."

"You look like a superhero," King said. "I'mma call you Runnin' Man."

"Yeah, like the dance?" Aunt Sophie asked.

"What dance?" I replied, totally confused.

"Doesn't matter," my mother cut in, now back to business. She grabbed her purse. "We gotta go."

We went dashing down the road toward the bus stop, only to see the bus pulling off just before we got there.

"No!" Mum shouted, turning toward me. I could tell she wanted to swear, but she didn't. She just bit her lip, then looked at me and said, "I'm so sorry, baby."

But it was okay. I had walked it so many times, and I knew that it was only like a fifteen-minute trek. With all the stops the bus was going to have to make along the way, we could probably get there quicker if we walked anyway. So I told them to follow me, as I took the short way, for once. Imagine it, my mother in yellow trousers with flowers all over them (not scrubs) and lipstick and red cheek stuff on her face, and my aunt with jeans and trainers, with a bright pink T-shirt and a baseball cap, and my cousin, King, dressed in shorts and a top and the same shoes as my beat-up ones, holding a big neon sign. Imagine the three of them, following behind me, Castle Cranshaw, dressed in an electric-blue track uniform. The Defender.

We walked past the fish market, the wig shop, and Everything Sports, before I realised that I had to make one quick stop. Mr Charles's store. Luckily, it sits right in the middle of everything. At least it seems like it does. Like I can always get to it no matter where I am in the city. I think maybe that was Mr Charles's plan. He's smart like that, and I can see it even if his family don't. He's the smartest person with a store in the whole city, and maybe even the world. That's what I think.

When we got there, I told Mum and Aunt Sophie and King to give me a second.

"Just need to get something," I explained.

I pushed the door open and there Mr Charles was, standing behind the counter as usual, staring at his television.

"Castle! How are you, my friend?" Mr Charles said, holding his hand out. "What's with the getup?"

"This is my uniform. The Defenders," I explained, pointing to the gold word printed across my chest.

"Who?" Mr Charles leaned in so he could hear me.

"The Defenders," I said louder. "The team I told you about. Today's my first race, and I just wanted you to see me." There was no way I could hide the excitement in my voice.

"Ahhh," Mr Charles flashed a huge smile. He grabbed a bag of sunflower seeds off the wall. "Then take these for good luck. Pretend they're power pills," he said, which I thought was funny because for me, they kinda were. At least in my head.

"Thanks, Mr Charles. I'll tell you how it goes," I said, reaching out for his hand.

"Yes, yes, please do, son," he practically shouted, squeezing my hand. "Now, get out of here. You can't be great if you're late!"

After four or five more minutes, my mother, my aunt, and my cousin and me came up on the park. I was used to seeing it sprinkled with only a few parents – mainly Lu's mum and a few others – and us, the runners on the track. But on race day, there were people everywhere. From the street, you could hear the buzz of the crowd and the sounds of whistles and you could see food trucks and all the different colour jerseys as coaches had their teams stretching and warming up. Once we got closer, I found my squad, that electric blue standing out.

"Ghost!" a voice came from behind me. It was Sunny.

"Sunny! Wassup, man?" We dapped. "This is my mum, and my aunt, and my cousin, King." Sunny shook everybody's hand, then told me to come get stretched and warmed up. My family lined up along the fence with who I guessed were the parents of the rest of my teammates. I saw Sunny's father, Mr Lancaster, still dressed up in a suit, but with sunglasses on. Patty's (white) mother, holding her little sister, Maddy, up on her shoulders. Lu's mum was there holding pom-poms, of course, and next to her was a man who looked just like Goose, the flashy dope man who hangs out at the basketball court. But it wasn't. At least I didn't think it was. Couldn't have been.

When Sunny and I got to where the rest of the team was, everyone was sitting down with their legs out in front of them, holding the tips of their feet and pulling. It hurts like crazy, but Coach said it was good for us. The team looked at me as I sat down. They all noticed the uniform. And the silver bullets. I was dressed. I was a Defender. I was ready.

"Okay," Coach said, needing to speak much louder than usual so that we could hear him over the noise. "I've got the lineup. Let's start with the distance race. Running the mile, we have Sunny for the guys. Lynn for the girls. For the eight hundred, Mikey, you're taking Chris's place. Outlaw, you're second heat. For the girls, Patty, you got this. Deja, you got second heat." When Coach got to the two hundred metre, he looked at me and Lu. Then he looked down at his clipboard. Then back at us.

"Lu, you're gonna take the two hundred," Coach said. "And the one hundred." Lu held back a smile and nodded. Coach got me. I thought he was going to let me run, but I guess this was the real last part of my punishment. I tried not to act disappointed. I looked over at my family. King and Aunt Sophie holding the sign, waiting to lift it into the air and scream like maniacs. And Ma. Standing there so proud of me.

"And Ghost," Coach said, glancing over at Coach Whit, then back at me. I snapped out of my trance. "You think you can handle the one hundred too?"

I grinned, and I couldn't get "yes" out of my mouth. Such a short, easy word, but I couldn't spit it out. So I just nodded, and swallowed the yes, hoping it might go down my throat, through my stomach, and down into my legs.

"We're not gonna run any relays or hurdles yet," Coach said. "This is the first meet, and we've got some work to do. But I'm watching every one of you, so let's get out there and burn."

We all went to the side of the track and waited for our races. Everyone was so hype, jumping around, trying to stay loose. Lu's mother came over and gave us a container full of orange slices, which I thought was super nice. But I didn't want any oranges. And I met Coach's wife, Mrs Margo, and his baby son, Tyrone. The crazy thing was, even though Coach was an Otis and a chipped-tooth turtle face, Mrs Margo was pretty. And so nice. She passed out Gatorades to everybody, but when she got to me, she thanked me for cleaning out Coach's cab. That made me feel real special. But I didn't really want no oranges or no Gatorade. I had my power pills. My sunflower seeds. I ran over to my mother, who had them tucked in her purse. She handed me the bag, then grabbed me and hugged me. Again.

"I'm so proud of you," she said. Then she caught me slipping and added, *"Ghost."* She must've heard Sunny say it or somebody, but she now knew my nickname – the name I gave myself – and judging from her bright smile, I think she liked it. I had no idea that being on a team would make her so lovey-dovey, but it was cool. It reminded me of how it used to be, back when we slept in our rooms and there was family pictures on the wall.

Back with the rest of the Defenders, I ate the sunflower seeds, one by one, waiting for my race. My chance. The first race was a relay. The boys 4 x 800. I got to just sit and watch to see how races really went down, since we weren't running relays. Runners from eight different teams all lined up in their lines, staggered at different starting points. The Bruisers, the Wings, and a bunch of other silly names that were nowhere near as dope as the Defenders. Everybody put one foot forward, just barely touching the line. They leaned in, some wiggling their fingers. Then – and this caught me totally off guard – there's a gunshot, which is the thing that tells you to go. I'll tell you one thing, it made me feel a little weird, but whoever invented track got the whole *gun means go* thing right.

The crowd started screaming as the boys burned the track up. One of the teams, I think they were called the Assassins, dropped the baton. It made a clinking sound, which in a nutshell, is what losing sounded like. It's hard to come back from that.

After the boys were the girls. Patty came over to me and told me how she felt like she could pretty much smoke all the girls out there. I believed her. Patty was definitely going to be a problem.

Next was the boys one-hundred-metre hurdle, which was the most exciting thing I had ever seen. It was crazy! I asked Coach if we were ever going to run hurdles, and he told me that we would, but that it takes some real work. He said the kids who left the team and went to high school – the kids whose spots we filled – were amazing hurdlers. Then he said he used to run hurdles, while tapping his hand on his chest, his secret tattooed Olympic medal. I told him I wanted to do it. He told me to focus on today.

Then came the girls' hurdles, which the crowd seemed to be into even more than the boys. Patty was jumping up and down screaming, because one of her friends was running. The girl didn't win first, but she did come in second, which wasn't bad.

And then came the one-hundred-metre sprint.

"Lu, Ghost," Coach called out. "Y'all ready?" Me and Lu nodded, and Coach said what he always said, this time with a returned nod. "On the line."

We stepped out on the track and walked down to the end. Lu's mum instantly started screaming and waving those stupid pom-poms. No clue what she was saying, but whatever it was, it was loud. Until, Aunt Sophie.

"C-A-S-T-L-E!" Aunt Sophie screamed. "Smoke 'em! Burn 'em! Dust 'em! Roast 'em!" she shrieked. It was like her and Lu's mum were a perfect out-of-control cheerleading pair. I looked over and King was holding the sign above his head. It said, CASTLE CRANSHAW AIN'T NO JOKE. YOU ARE! Nice.

All the runners from all the different teams were slapping hands, when I saw . . . him. No way. No. Freakin'. Way. He ran? He *ran*? By now you know who I'm talking about. Brandon Simmons. He was standing in lane eight, running for a team that called themselves the Bolts. He saw me the same time I saw him, and he looked just as shocked as I was.

"You run?" I asked, coming toward him. *Brandon was a runner?* He was tall enough to play ball, so I always assumed that's what he did. Then again, I should've known better, because he had those slimy hands. Can't hold no ball with those butter fingers.

"You run?" he responded, wiping his hands ironically on his shorts. Then he smirked and shot breath out his nose like he couldn't believe it. Like I was some kind of joke. Like he didn't see that sign King was holding up.

"Yeah," Lu said from behind me. He put his hand on my shoulder. "He runs, real, real, real fast," he said, taunting Brandon. Lu pulled me into him, grabbed me by the back of my neck. "It's me and you," he said, snapping me out of my Brandon Simmons nightmare state and back into focus. Had I known Brandon was a runner, I would've told Dre and Red to come to the meet just so they could see me smoke him. Shoot, I might've invited the whole school. Even Principal Marshall. Maybe even would've told Shamika to bring that laugh with her for this special occasion. Lu gave me five, then repeated, "It's me" – he pointed to himself – "and you." He put his finger on my chest.

I was in lane six, Lu in lane one. I bent down, untied my silver shoes, then retied them.

I looked around at the crowd, a smear of people rooting for their friend or son or brother or teammate. Somebody was probably there even rooting for Brandon. Then I looked over at the side where the Defenders were, Coach clapping, a proud grin on his face. Sunny cheering, an orange slice in his mouth, the peel like a bright mouthpiece. And Patty – who by the way had on shiny lip stuff and had her hair greased and slicked straight back – squatted down and stared, almost like she was mind-beaming speed to me. She nodded. I nodded. My mother, looking at me with wet eyes. She waved. And all I could think about at that moment was the two of us running down the hall three years ago.

"On your mark!" said the starter. My heart *thump-thumped, thump-thumped,* and I could feel my insides turning colours. I'm not sure what colour. Not red. Not blue. Something else. Something different. A colour I never felt before. I squatted down, pushed my feet back against the blocks, stretched out my thumbs and index fingers and placed them on the edge of the white starting line. Rested my weight on my arms.

ACKNOWLEDGEMENTS

A special thanks goes out to my amazing editor, Caitlyn Dlouhy, for her constant encouragement. The same goes for my agent, Elena Giovinazzo. You both are fantastic collaborators, and even better friends. Thank you to my school track coaches, Coach Chris and Coach Williams, and all the people on my team who were so much better than me. Seriously. To my man, Mike Posey, for helping with all the track details I'd forgotten. And lastly, but most importantly, to all the young people who are running . . . may this be book be breath.

JASON REYNOLDS
Author

Jason is a critically acclaimed writer and poet and the winner of more than 25 US and International awards including the 2018 Edgar Award, Newbery Honor, Printz Honor, and twice winner of the Walter Dean Myers Award. You can find his ramblings at
JASONWRITESBOOKS.COM

SELOM SUNU
Illustrator

Selom is a devoted Christian working as a Character Designer and Illustrator. He currently lives in the UK with his wife and daughter. There are many sources of inspiration for Selom's work and he often thinks of the characteristics and features of family members when designing characters.

GUINNESS WORLD RECORDS

The Guinness World Records first began in 1954 and was run by two brothers, Norris and Ross, from London as a fun fact-finding agency.

Did you know that the longest race ever staged was for 525 hours 57 mins and 20 seconds and went from New York City to Los Angeles?

Usain Bolt is the first man ever to hold Olympic Gold and World Championship Gold at the two sprint distances of 100m and 200m!

The tallest sunflower grown measures 9.17 metres and was grown by Hans-Peter Schiffer in Germany.

HELLO FROM KOHQ*!

Thanks for reading GHOST we really hope you enjoyed it.

KNIGHTS OF is all about YOU. We make books for every kind of reader, from every kind of background and hope you'll read more of the great stories we publish. If it's fearless knights riding bikes or solving mysteries with your sister, if great stories are what you're after - we've got them!

Run to the next page to find out what the next book on the RUN series is.

*Knights Of Headquarters

READ THE REST OF
THE *RUN* SERIES:

PATINA
SUNNY
LU

COMING SOON
TO A BOOKSHOP
NEAR YOU!